For Gail —

I hope you enjoy meeting Harry + Sophie as much as I have enjoyed meeting you!

Enjoy the book,

Paul

FIVE DAYS IN MAY

The Brookfield Murders

A HARRISON HUNT MYSTERY

by

PAUL EISEMAN

authorHOUSE®

AuthorHouse™
1663 Liberty Drive, Suite 200
Bloomington, IN 47403
www.authorhouse.com
Phone: 1-800-839-8640

First published by AuthorHouse   4/10/2009

ISBN: 978-1-4389-5957-3 (sc)
ISBN: 978-1-4389-5958-0 (hc)

Library of Congress Control Number: 2009902839

Printed in the United States of America
Bloomington, Indiana

CHAPTER
1

As USUAL, I HAD A splitting headache. I always expect my right temple to remind me of the tensions and exasperations looming ahead of me as I embark on each new project, but on this particular Saturday morning the headache was worse than anticipated. To make it even worse, the dull throbbing was accompanied by a curious queasiness in my midsection, as though I had eaten or imbibed much too sybaritically the night before and was now paying the price for my self-indulgence. However, since I had not particularly overdone it at last night's dinner party, the butterflies in my tummy surprised me and added to the annoyance I was feeling.

"One more cross to bear I suppose," I sighed with barely a half smile as I took one last appraising look at myself in the full length mirror. Mostly satisfied with the general image reflecting back at me and ignoring the slightly paunchy way my new cashmere sweater rose up to remind me of past indiscretions, I crossed to the desk and once again looked over the list that accompanied the photographs.

Sophie had done her usual impeccable job of typing each person's name precisely next to each ten-minute time slot. Therefore, at the rate of six per hour, I would be face to face with eighteen smiling and slightly perspiring faces this morning and, following a much needed and anticipated lunch break, thirty more this afternoon. About the same daunting number of appointments was scheduled for tomorrow as well. "Why must I put myself through this torture?" I only half jokingly asked myself as I quickly perused today's glossies one final time and then putting all the paperwork into my new buttery-soft attaché case (a gift from an admirer as was, incidentally, the previously noted cashmere), downed two bubbling Alka Seltzer tablets, waved beneficently to the mousey young woman at the front desk, and departed *posthaste* the sanctity of the Inn for the twenty minute drive to the theater and the imminent encounters with those forty-eight doubtlessly capped and needy smiles.

I suppose that morning's journey through the rural lanes and rustic vistas of Brookfield should have put me in a more congenial frame of mind. I suppose the ever present views of Macintosh red barns surrounded by pastoral green and yellow fields that whizzed by me should have warmed my innards with a Grant Woodish, heart-tugging, throat-lumping appreciation for that ever-touted Nature. I suppose the clapboard clanking of the last covered bridge in that part of the state under my rental car's tires and the bucolic bleating of woolly farmyard critters in my ears should have lightened my spirit and brought a noble savage glow to my urban sensibilities. However, I'm afraid that all I thought about was how ineffective that Alka Seltzer was and how much I needed a massive jolt of caffeine.

Turning into the parking lot of the rather folksy-looking but not unattractive barnlike structure at which I was contractually bound to spend the summer, I was relieved to see that Sophie's familiar pumpkin colored beetle was reassuringly parked among the large number of other vehicles. Displeased that I was not able to find a space closer to the theater's front door, I begrudgingly trudged across the gravel surface and entered.

Although the auditions were not to begin for almost an hour, the theater's lobby was aswarm with men and women of all sizes and shapes milling about or sitting rather stiffly in the folding chairs provided for them. Not surprised that at first glance none of them seemed recognizable from his or her submitted photo, I was a bit taken aback by the sudden hush that greeted my entrance through the theater's massive wooden door. All sets of eyes instantly glued themselves to mine as one by one those familiar and expected fawning smiles appeared on the faces of the eager actors. If I had been casting the role of Uriah Heep, I would have had some difficulty in choosing the most unctuous candidate.

I attempted to present as pleasant a mien as possible to the madding crowd as I threaded my way between them and seemingly nonchalantly entered the auditorium closing its door quickly behind me.

"My God, Sophie, what a throng! What have we gotten ourselves into this time?"

Of course I was aware that I had only erupted in this over the top fashion in order that Sophie would, as always, calmly assuage my nerves and rationally present things in their most positive light. Of course I was also aware that Sophie fully understood this need of mine and was willing to respond accordingly. We had played this unspoken game for too many years to stop at this juncture. So, after patiently reminding me of the creative opportunities this summer promised and that we would both have the pleasure of seeing and working with Charlie Wetherstone again, and after pouring me a steaming cup of her freshly brewed coffee, I found myself in a much better state of mind, and we were ready to get down to business. I only wished that my head and stomach had improved as much as my mood.

Removing from my left shoe the last of the parking lot's irritating pebbles, I briefly glanced at the handouts Sophie had prepared for the auditioning actors. As usual, she had clearly and concisely covered all the main points. The actors had been selected by a local casting agent to compete to be members of a summer repertory company at the theater. The company would perform two new plays which I would direct. By the way, I had also written these plays and was anxious to work out any kinks that might be found in the scripts. The theater had been awarded a state grant to produce new works and hire an outside writer/director for the project. Since I had a more than modest reputation as an innovative New York theater director and incipient playwright, my application and scripts had readily been accepted by the theater's quite clearly astute board. The chance to work with a New York director had obviously been the motivation for the extra nervousness apparent in the local actors I had seen in the lobby.

Accustomed to working with more seasoned New York City actors, I had been a bit hesitant to work with unknown talent, but the opportunity this project offered me was more than enough for me to take the risk.

The plan was for each actor to perform a short monologue of the actor's choice that showed his or her facility with elevated language. Those actors who showed potential would also be asked to read short sides from the scripts. The sides and the handouts had been given to the actors by the casting agent several days ago.

Sophie was now carefully reading each actor's resumé and highlighting information that she knew would be of interest to me. Watching how focused she was with this task reminded me how grateful I was to have Sophie in my life. We had met at Yale Drama School. I had been a promising directing major and Sophia Anastasia Xerxes was a youngish member of the dean's office staff. Sophie X, as she was affectionately called, and I hit it off right away and kept in touch after I left New Haven. I heard she was moving to the City about the same time I got a big directing break there, and I was delighted when she accepted my offer to be my assistant. We have now worked together on and off for over twenty years and have developed a warm friendship. Never married and by no means a raving beauty, Sophie always, I guessed, had a bit of a crush on me, but she has accepted my decision that our relationship could only be platonic. Sophie X was my Ann Sothern, my Rosalind Russell, my gal Friday. If I were not her Cary Grant, perhaps I was her George Sanders or her Brian Donlevy. In any case, I felt she considered me a respected colleague and good friend. We understood each other and, though she insisted I was at times a maddeningly difficult person to work with, we usually made a very good team.

"You haven't touched any of those especially gooey pastries I brought you, Harry. Anything wrong with my choice? Or," she smiled ironically, "heaven be praised, have you finally decided to eat more sensibly?"

I reacted to Sophie's dig with a raised eyebrow and an admission that the current uneasy state of my solar plexus would be even more imperiled by ingesting my usual breakfast of choice, however tempting the Danish and donuts looked.

With a sympathetic shrug and an offer of two antacid tablets, which I readily accepted, Sophie resumed her professional manner.

"I starred ten of today's resumés, seven men and three women. They look like they might have the background to do the job. Also," Sophie gave me a meaningful look, "did you happen to notice that Belinda Bobbie is scheduled for 2:40?"

"Yes," I whispered and returned Sophie's pointed look. "At least I have all morning and luncheon to decide how I shall handle that meeting." Remembering the last time we had seen Belinda sent chills down both our spines; at least it did mine.

CHAPTER 2

ON THAT OMINOUS NOTE AND after synchronizing our watches, I assumed my position behind the table provided for me, and with a snappy salute Sophie marched out to the lobby to start the proceedings. Quickly popping one more tablet from the bottle Sophie had thoughtfully left for me, I prepared for the worst. I was not disappointed.

To begin with, the first four actors one after another delivered monologues that were at best mediocre (the impossibly chipper Suzie McKenzie's Ophelia and the over the top macho Chuck Palumbo's Petruccio) and at worst embarrassingly pretentious (the absurdly dramatic Benton Burnett's Henry V and the simperingly saccharine Mitzi Malone's —I almost barfed- Lady Macbeth).

"Out, out, damned spots before my eyes!" I mentally moaned, as the coyly grinning Lady M coquettishly departed.

With all good reason then I found it difficult to be more than perfunctorily cordial to the several members of the theater's board of directors when they perkily poked their heads in for a moment to wish me good luck. They were apparently going to hold a board meeting somewhere in the theater's back rooms.

At this point my stomach and headache were even worse, so I ordered the bemused Sophie to remove the breakfast pastries from my sight and nostrils. The ordinarily tempting aroma was beginning to nauseate me, and their sugary sweetness evoked too painfully the memory of Ms. Mitzi's astonishing performance.

Barely looking at the next actor when he entered the room, I phlegmatically greeted him with my standard opening pleasantry, "And how are you today, uh… Randy?" I was unprepared for the torrent of words that tumbled out of his mouth.

"Actually, I'm pretty freaking terrified, sir. Having the chance to read for the great Harrison Hunt has me scared shitless! Oh Christ, pardon my French. Being cast this summer would be an awesome opportunity for me, AWESOME, and I don't want to screw it up. I've read everything that's been written about you, and I've seen the work you've gotten out of other actors, and I know how much I could learn from you. Jeez, I'm sweating bullets here!"

"By the gods, finally an honest man! Good for you!" I practically shouted.

When Randy gave me a perplexed look, I explained to him that it was not unreasonable that actors would be nervous at auditions that meant something to them. However the others I had seen that morning had made the terrible mistake to try to pretend they felt otherwise. By attempting to appear calm and even a bit blasé, they denied their real feelings and short-circuited any possibility that they could give authentic, truthful performances. Any unique talents and special qualities they might have were doomed to remain hidden under the artifice of their smiling but false exteriors. By concentrating so hard on their pose of not appearing anxious (as they assumed that would appear "amateurish") they doomed themselves to performances that were at best technical. I'm always looking for actors who truthfully present who they are and how their characters are really feeling. I believe that truth can only come from truth. If an actor works from a lie, it is impossible for him or her to perform authentically.

Randy's response to my oration was to exhale forcefully an extremely audible and surprisingly high pitched sigh of relief that caused both of us to chuckle a little. The blush that then covered his face went hand in hand with the exponential growth of his pleasant grin causing him to appear even more likeable and open.

"Whoooeee, that sure takes a load off, Mr. Hunt," the carrot-topped, lanky, Lacrosse playing, t-shirt wearing, twenty-five year old Randy Williamson spouted.

"I'm very glad to hear it. Do you feel like doing your monologue for me now?"

"I sure do, Mr. Hunt. Thanks."

Freed a bit from his fears and wisely allowing any nerves that did remain to inform his performance, Mr. Williamson comically and rather touchingly did a nice job of presenting Lysander's gushing declarations of puppy love from "A Midsummer Night's Dream." I was equally pleased with his reading from the sides he had been given. With a firm handshake and with his very pearly whites lighting the way, Randy left the audition as happy as I was.

Yes, happy. It is a misconception and disservice to themselves for actors to think of directors as the enemy relishing any chance to criticize, reject and destroy them. In fact, I (and I would think all good directors) hope that every actor auditioning would give a brilliant performance, that every actor auditioning would be perfect for the role and aid the director in achieving his vision. The director hopes to deliver an excellent production and, the more good actors he sees, the better the chance that this goal would be reached. A director is actually disappointed when an actor auditions badly. Unfortunately, I was fated to endure many more of those disappointments that weekend.

Of the eighteen morning faces and voices that blurred into one large indistinguishable disappointment, only four actors stood out clearly in my mind. In addition to Randy Williamson, I enjoyed the honest performances of one other man and two women. It takes a lot of courage to bare oneself truthfully to a stranger instead of presenting a safer, "professional" image. I looked forward to meeting these four actors again in the callbacks scheduled for Tuesday evening.

The final morning audition was one of the few good ones. As a result, I felt a little better as Sophie came in to see me. I was ready to enjoy a quiet lunch break with her but was surprised to hear her say, "Harry, I hate to tell you this, but there's a guy out in the lobby who wants to talk with you." She silenced my objection with these words: "His name is Robert Gregory, and he's Belinda Bobbie's brother. He seems like a decent guy, and he's pleading with me for a few words with you now. I think you should see him. What do you say?"

Knowing Sophie's basic good sense and general lack of sentimentality, I quieted my misgivings and agreed to see him. I asked Sophie to sit in as well, in case the meeting grew disagreeable.

While Sophie left to usher Mr. Gregory in, my mind went back to the first time I had met his sister. It was hard to believe that it was over fifteen years ago that Belinda Bobbie first walked into my life. Or rather than *walk*, a far more fitting verb to describe how Belinda entered a room and a person's consciousness would have to be *strut*. Staggeringly beautiful, her long blond hair floating behind her, Belinda instantly attracted the attention, admiration, envy or lust of everyone at the cocktail party given in my honor. Her confident, intelligent royal blue eyes took in the room as a whole and then focused on me. It was a bit disconcerting to receive the force of that penetrating look, and, though intrigued and flattered, "a cold perspiration bespangled" my "brow." The lyric from "The Mikado" sung at that very instant by the singer/pianist seated across the room so accurately described my condition that I was forced to chuckle ironically.

"Do I make you smile so beguilingly?" Belinda's silken voice questioned me. At that moment I was lost. Of course I knew who Belinda Bobbie was; everyone did. She was the toast of the town, the actress everyone wanted to see and be seen with. The off-Broadway sensation whose performance had single handedly propelled her show to Broadway and a stunning success. Scripts and offers were flying into her hands. If Belinda Bobbie agreed to be in your show, you had it made. And this gorgeous, successful, talented, powerhouse of a woman was speaking to me and staring into my eyes as if I were the only one in the room.

As Sophie opened the door for Robert Gregory, something in his face instantly reminded me of the *last* time Belinda had looked into my eyes. Although she was then hysterical and babbling incoherently and completely unable to stand erect, her eyes, like her brother's now three years later, for a long moment looked into mine with the deepest, most ineffable sadness.

"Hello, Mr. Hunt. Thank you very much for seeing me." Robert Gregory's soft-spoken voice corresponded to the sadness and weariness in his face and body. He seemed a man who had been so buffeted by life's cruel realities that he would no longer have the strength or even the will to continue fighting against them. Usually such apparent weakness or resignation irritated me, but strangely I felt only instant sympathy for this man who appeared much older than his years. I gave a quick look to Sophie acknowledging that she had been correct in asking me to see him. I think I knew why Robert Gregory had come to the theater and, with a sinking feeling in my gut, dreaded the very good possibility of having to hurt him.

"Not at all," I replied. "Would you like to take a seat, Mr. Gregory?"

"No thanks. I'd rather stand if you don't mind. I don't want to take any more of your time than...Mr. Hunt, I've come here to ask you, to beg you to..." Once again, he interrupted himself. Silently, he began to pace back and forth before Sophie and me. Then, as he slowly resumed speaking, his movements mirrored his disjointed words. His steps were first short and rapid. Then they became more measured and deliberate. Then he began to circle us in a slow, rambling fashion. It was both disconcerting and pitiable to witness the obvious difficulty he was having in finding the right words to express his thoughts. The hood attached to the loose fitting sweatshirt he wore bobbed a bit behind him as he jerkily kept moving around us.

"Mr. Hunt, Mr. Hunt, my big sister was everything to me... I adored her... and after our mother died, she became like a ... Our dad was so devastated that he was unable to take very good care of us. It was little eight-year old Belinda who became the mother figure. I was only three when our mom died and it was Belinda, beautiful, beautiful Belinda who like an angel...She was so good, so unselfish, so giving, so beautiful. She sacrificed so much for me that when she...I was so proud of her success, her talent, she had worked so hard and when she became a genuine star, I knew it was only right that such an angel would become a star, a beautiful, beautiful star.. and then she met *him*. Like Belinda, I thought he was as wonderful as she. I thought she had finally found the happiness she deserved. I was thrilled when they married and now it seemed that she had everything, a marvelous career, a loving husband. But then, as you of course know, everything fell apart...She never blamed him, you know. She blamed only herself... she wouldn't allow me to say one bad word against him...and after that terrible, terrible night..." he groaned pretty loudly then, and I suddenly realized he had been softly moaning to himself all the time that he had been speaking.

"Excuse me, Mr. Hunt, I'm not feeling so good."

"Can I get you something? A glass of water?"

"No thanks, I'll be all right. I guess talking about ... this... makes me feel like someone, something's kicking me in the..." he groaned again, but silenced Sophie and me as we started to rise.

"No, please, let me finish what I have to say. Then I'll be able to get some rest. I can use some rest."

He began moving again as he continued speaking. "So... after that terrible night, I knew it was *my* turn, that it was only right that now I become the parent, that it was only right that I take care of Belinda, as she had taken care of me as a kid. AND IT WORKED!" There was suddenly a gleam in his tortured eyes. "She has come back to me, to us, Mr. Hunt, to the world. She found the strength again, she found the courage again, she licked it, Mr. Hunt. And I ask you, I beg you to be the one to give her another chance. Please, please give her another chance, let her prove to the world that she is back, that she can be the star, the angel she was. Please, please cast her in your show and I know, I guarantee she will make you proud, make herself proud, make me..." Suddenly, with a horrifying groan, clutching his stomach, Robert Gregory fell to the ground in front of me and was still.

CHAPTER

3

"MY GOD, HARRY. IS HE dead?" Sophie whispered. We both stared as if paralyzed at Robert Gregory's lifeless body.

I could neither answer her nor move from my chair for what seemed like hours, but was actually only a matter of seconds, when, suddenly, I thought I saw… could it be?… no, it was only a trick of my eyes, only wishful thinking, but … yes, the corpse *had* moved! I definitely saw his right foot twitch slightly.

This apparent miracle stirred me out of my immobility. I bent down and quickly felt for his pulse. I had seen enough "Law and Order" episodes to know how to do this (despite my insistent claim that I never watched anything but PBS). The pulse was found; he was still alive; time was of the essence; we sprang into action.

While I reached for my cellular phone in order to call 911, Sophie ran out to the lobby. I impatiently listened to the infernal ringtone while the phone took its own sweet time reawakening. Never before had the Fifth Brandenburg Concerto seemed so irritating. "Now what?" I muttered as the damned phone languidly searched for a signal. The wait was maddening. I remembered the impatience I felt at last night's dinner party when my phone failed to snag a signal. This was infinitely worse. Would the man on the floor lose his battle for life because of the technological ineptitude of Ma Bell, or whatever she was now called after divestiture. Would I be fated to be cast in the insignificant role of the silent spectator, the extraneous extra, the superfluous supernumerary lurking in the background helplessly waiting for the leading actor to enter and perform his heroic actions? Would I forever be the barb of late-night comics' jokes, or even worse, by *Variety*? Would I be derided as Hamlet without a Fifth Act, or even worse, as a buffoonish, inept, sanctimonious Polonius? And all because this damned phone would only endlessly continue *Searching for Network* whatever the hell that meant.

Fortunately, I was interrupted from this mental flagellation by Sophie's hurried return accompanied, surprisingly, by people, many people.

In the crowded confusion that ensued, I could only hear snippets of sound bites:

"There he is, doctor, please hurry." That definitely was Sophie's voice.

"Ohhhh Noooo!" The horrified scream came from someone else. I don't think it was from me.

"Move aside." "Don't push." "Give him some breathing space." Three new voices.

"Please, everyone, clear the room so I can do my work." A male voice I vaguely recognized.

"Come on, Harry, let's go into the lobby." Sophie's voice again, her hand on my arm.

My senses continued being bombarded: the solid slamming of the auditorium door behind us, the sudden relative coolness of the lobby, the sweet smell of a vaguely familiar perfume, the taste of the paper cup brushing my lips, the hoarseness in my throat soothed a little by the water, the muffled sound of a siren growing louder and louder, the shuddering of the front door as it was pushed open, the squeals of the gurney's wheels pleading for oil, the cacophony of multiple shoes making a hurried exit, that siren again. Then blessed silence.

As my heart rate slowed to a manageable level, I noticed that Sophie was talking to me again. "I bet you could use a drink. I sure as hell could." She then sighed mightily while luxuriantly stretching like a tabby cramped too long in a carrier.

"I think I'm still in a daze, Sophie. Everything happened so quickly. Who in the name of Beelzebub were all those people, and where did they come from? How did you get a doctor to appear so quickly?"

"They're the theater's board members who luckily were still in the green room when I rushed in there. Dr. Freemount is on the board. We met him last night at the dinner party, and he very professionally took over when I told him about Robert Gregory, who happens to be his patient. There are evidently some advantages to living in a small town. The doctor immediately surmised what the problem was. In fact, everyone seemed to know Gregory, and they were very concerned about his welfare. So the entire board rushed in causing some confusion and getting in the doctor's way a bit until he banished everyone to the lobby. They all left when the ambulance arrived. Belinda rode in the back of the ambulance with the doctor."

"Oh my God, I thought I recognized that perfume."

"Didn't you see her? She arrived at the theater during the confusion unaware of what had happened to her brother. I don't think I'll ever forget the sound of her scream when she saw him lying there."

"As if she needed any new troubles," I said softly then asked, "Did you find out what caused Robert Gregory's collapse?"

"Nope. The ambulance left too quickly to get a chance to talk with the doctor. But that Mrs.-oh what's her name? - that nipped and tucked Brahman on the board, the one with that necklace?"

"Bitsie Adams," I chuckled as Sophie's hand gesture perfectly illustrated the massive size of that dazzling chunk of jewelry.

"Right, well I overheard that battleaxe mentioning something about diabetes."

"Well, I'm sure we'll hear more soon. All in all, the perfect ending to a perfect morning," I moaned. "Do you think it's appropriate to continue the afternoon auditions?"

Sophie gave me that meaningful look of hers again. "You know, Harry, what a tight schedule we're on. But it all depends on how you're feeling, whether or not you're up to it. How's your stomach doing?"

Strange to say, I had forgotten all about my symptoms in the light of the chaotic commotion. "Actually, I feel less discomfort than I did this morning."

"Then I suggest we continue. There's still about forty minutes before you see the next actor. I noticed a little kitchen back in the green room. Why don't we see if we can rustle up a little lunch and then push on?"

Sophie performed more of her usual magic. We munched on some very decent (but bland in consideration of my tummy) chicken salad she whipped up, and I was safely ensconced at my station in the theater in time for actor number nineteen.

And actor twenty, and twenty-one, and on and on throughout the long afternoon. Many of the auditions lasted no more than seven or eight minutes. Usually, I can determine within the first thirty seconds of an actor's reading whether or not he or she is of interest to me. As in all introductions, first impressions are vitally important and very difficult to amend.

Once again, only about one out of five of the men and women I met that afternoon made enough of a good impression with their monologues to be asked to read from the new scripts and then be considered for the all important final callbacks on Tuesday.

The only break I had from the grueling schedule was at 2:40 when Belinda Bobbie failed to appear. This of course was to be expected. She obviously was still at the hospital with her brother. Although I empathized with the new catastrophe in her life, I must admit that I also experienced a sense of relief when Sophie and not Belinda entered the auditorium and sat down next to me.

"How you doing?" She knew how drained I would be at this point and how much I would appreciate the fresh cup of coffee she brought me. "I'm afraid there's only half a donut left out there from the box this morning. Would you like it, or shall I try to find other sweets from the kitchen for you?"

"No thanks, sweet thing, the coffee is fine. I assume there are no other cancellations for the remainder of the day?"

"No rest for the wicked, I'm afraid." Sophie then edged her chair closer to mine and lowered her normally booming voice to a conspiratorial whisper. "Listen, Harry, the buzz from the actors this afternoon was all about Robert Gregory and you. How your quick thinking may have saved his life."

I shot her a withering glance. "Sophie, you know as well as I that I was not of the slightest assistance to that poor young man. In fact, I regret to say, just the opposite."

"Well, whether you were or not, the town sure seems to think so. You must have noticed an even greater amount of hero worship than usual from the actors."

"It's extremely difficult to ascertain whether their admiration is genuine or they're merely trying to suck up. Brownie points, we used to call them, I believe."

Sophie's boisterous laugh was, as always, infectious and helped to assuage the twinge of shame I was feeling. Looking at her watch, she shifted to her professional persona.

"Well, with that happy note, our break I'm sad to say is over. So, I'll refill your coffee cup, give you a peck on your chubby little cheek, square my shoulders and return to the war zone."

As she left, I thought I heard her say, "Once more unto the breach!" I had only a minute or so to resume my directorial demeanor before the next applicant entered.

The remaining few hours of the auditions seemed to drag interminably, and my neck was quite stiff from sitting so long in one position as the final actress of the day reluctantly closed the door behind her wiping a residual pretty tear from her pretty cheek. She apparently had been much moved by her maudlin monologue. I unfortunately had not.

I printed a large red "No" next to her name (Could she really have been christened Lori Lee Lawrence? If so, what had her parents been thinking or, more possibly, been smoking?) and looked one more time at the list. Of the forty-seven actors I had seen, I had ten marked as probable callbacks. I marveled once again at Sophie's perspicacity as I noted that these were the same ten Sophie had selected from their resumés this morning. Feeling a little redundant, I rotated my neck several times till I heard the reassuring crack and crossed to the door to rejoin Sophie in the lobby.

At the exact moment I reached the door, it magically opened seemingly by itself, and I was suddenly face to face with those royal blue eyes I could never forget.

CHAPTER 4

IT WAS A DARK AND stormy night.

No, that won't work.

How about: It was the best of times, it was the worst of times...?

Or: Call me Ishmael?

Or: Marley was dead?

Or: In a hole in the ground there lived a hobbit ?

Or how about: Lolita, light of my life, fire of my loins? Hmmm ...actually that's closest to the way I felt when I saw Belinda again. But enough horseplay. Enough procrastination. I begrudgingly decided to take a sober approach to my onerous task and not jokingly plagiarize a famous first line to begin my journal. But, instead, perfunctorily start with the date and place. I presume the police will appreciate that.

Okay, here goes:

Wednesday, May 14th
Pemberley Cottage
Brookfield

I have been asked to record my recollections of the events of the last few days, and I have decided to do so in the form of a journal.

I shall begin with my meeting with Belinda Bobbie on Saturday, May 10th a bit after 6:00 pm in the auditorium of the Brookfield Players' Barn Theater.

Oh, my God, how can I put down in a pedestrian, matter of fact way the emotions I felt when I saw and smelled and touched her again? How can I express in words the sensations that the sound of her voice rekindled in me?

Well, how about this:

I was a bit nervous to see Ms. Bobbie. It had been three years since we last set eyes on each other. Because of our unfortunate last meeting, I was unsure how to talk to her, as I was unsure how she felt about me. Since her mental instability had forced me to fire her from the Broadway play I was directing and since I had understood she had been quite ill, I was apprehensive about how our conversation would unfold.

But I was pleased to find that the relationship between Ms. Bobbie and myself was once again on the cordial and professional level it had always been before her illness. She graciously thanked me for aiding her brother a few hours before and hoped we could work together on the new project at this theater. I told her I would certainly consider her, and we shook hands as friends once again.

Well, as Joe Friday of the L.A. police department would say, those were "just the facts, ma'am." And they would just have to suffice for the Brookfield police department. But how well I knew that this sketchy description of our lengthy talk was merely the superficial tip of the iceberg. An iceberg that, at least on my part, was rapidly melting without any assistance from global warming.

What did I omit? How about the way Belinda chose to begin our conversation? She used the exact same words she had first uttered to me when we had met many years before: "Do *I* make you smile so beguilingly?" But this time instead of a glittery smile and a low adorable laugh the words were accompanied by tears flowing from her still incredible eyes. And definitely not the false crocodile tears Ms. Lori Lee had recently manufactured.

I then asked Sophie, who was standing immediately in back of Belinda, to leave us. She did so with a questioning look. Belinda and I sat in the last row of the orchestra seats and *remembered.*

Not just reminisced, but remembered totally every aspect of those glorious years we worked and played together. And remembered totally every detail of the tragedy that ended everything. We needed only the smallest phrase, the most succinct and telling gesture or sound or expression to bring it all back to us: the good and the bad. And we were closer than ever before.

She was her old self again. Or perhaps not. She was certainly still a most attractive woman with much of the old magic, but she was quieter than before and less demonstrative. She was simpler and calmer and much more open and, because of this, more beautiful than ever.

And when she quietly related her experiences of the past three years, the last of my resistance evaporated.

Though I didn't promise her anything, I knew she would be in this production and would illuminate it with a luster she had never shown before. And I knew I would do anything to keep her in my life again. I had let myself lose her once but vowed never to allow this to happen again.

... we shook hands as friends once again.

Well, yes, we did indeed shake hands but only in front of Dr. Freemount after Sophie had admitted him into the auditorium.

At the hospital, the good doctor had looked for Belinda to keep her abreast of recent developments. When a nurse advised him that she had called a cab to take her back to the theater, he drove the short distance back here to see how she was doing. Belinda had told me how much she had valued the friendship and assistance of the doctor and his wife after she had moved back to live with her brother. Both she and I were grateful that he had come in person to tell her the good news. Robert had taken a turn for the better and was now off the critical list.

I was overjoyed to see the sparkle that returned to her eyes when she heard these happy words. She wanted to return immediately to see him, but Doctor Freemount advised her Robert was still under sedation and she would do better to try to get a good night's sleep at home. So, thanking the doctor once again and looking once more deeply into my eyes, Belinda shook hands with me and went out to her car she had left in the parking lot earlier in the day.

When I turned back to the doctor, I noticed that both he and Sophie were looking at me curiously.

"And how are you doing after your long and difficult day, Mr. Hunt?" Dr. Freemount inquired. "You look pretty exhausted yourself and rather pale."

I started to demur, but Sophie interrupted me. "As a matter of fact, doctor, I've been rather worried about the boss myself. He's been complaining of stomach troubles and a bad headache all day. And added to the terrible shock when Mr. Gregory collapsed..."

"Now, Sophie, don't overdramatize. We'll just go back to the Inn and get a bite, and I'm sure I'll be feeling all bright and bushy-tailed in the morning."

"The Inn, hmmm?" The doctor amusingly allowed himself a more than slight shudder. "After sampling the far from sumptuous catering of the Inn's kitchen at last night's party and having heard tales of the less than five-star comfiness of its rooms, I think you'd be better served to go elsewhere. And a number of my patients have recently complained of a nasty stomach virus that's going around. We don't want our famous guest director to be in less than fine fettle this summer. It's important to the board and the community as a whole for the shows to be great successes. We don't want anything to prevent that from happening."

"Well, that's awfully nice of you to say this, Dr. Freemount…"

"Augie, please. And may I call you Harrison?"

"If you like…uh, Augie. But my friends call me Harry."

"Well, Harry. I suggest that you and Ms Xerxes move out of your rooms at the Inn and bunk in with my wife and me at our little cottage in the country. It's quiet and peaceful, and Louise is a marvelous cook, if I say so myself. We'll both be happy to give you all the TLC you can handle."

"Oh, we couldn't impose on you like that," Sophie said not too convincingly.

"I won't take no for an answer. It will certainly be our pleasure. Come on, let's get you all packed up, so you'll be in fine form for the long day of auditions tomorrow. What do you say, Harry?"

The inducements of a quiet room with a comfortable bed and good home cooking certainly sounded appealing, so we quickly agreed, and Sophie and I followed Dr. Freemount, I mean Augie, back to the Inn.

We were a bit surprised at how reluctant the mousey little receptionist was for us to move out. It seemed our staying at the Inn had added a lot to its stature, and she and the manager, who also tried to make a pitch for our remaining as guests, seemed quite genuinely disappointed at our departure.

Oh, well. Into every life a little rain must fall. Perhaps our dissatisfaction with the accommodations would give the owners and staff the prod they needed to improve. In a short hour we had packed, checked out and followed the doctor's car through winding roads and apple blossomed fields to their "modest little cottage."

I use that term only in the most ironic sense. Pemberley Cottage was a large and remarkably beautiful Victorian home. Driving up its red maple-lined curving driveway, we were surprised by the tasteful elegance of its porch-fronted exterior and more than delighted by the understated beauty of its interior.

Another lovely addition to the home was Mrs. Freemount. Louise, as she quickly insisted we call her, was very attractive, very sweet, and seemed to be delighted that we were to be her guests. She seemed to be a few years younger than her husband and me but had the poise and charm that seemed appropriate for the hostess of this charming house. Although I didn't remember meeting her at our welcoming party last night at the Inn, she seemed to remind me of someone. But the thought vanished from my mind as we sat down to a luscious dinner.

Augie had not been exaggerating when he had complimented his wife's cooking. From this meal it was clear that she was an expert in the culinary arts. The move to Pemberley Cottage seemed more and more fortuitous. Adding to this, the good fortune of seeing Belinda again and the apparently happy outcome of her brother's attack all made me think that, while the summer had begun so alarmingly, it now promised to be a very bright and happy one indeed. After all hadn't I just remarked that into every life some rain must fall? The rain clouds had indeed seemed to have blown merrily away. Hardly a dark and stormy night!

My assistant Sophia Xerxes and I accepted Dr. Freemount's gracious invitation to stay at his home. Our first night there was relaxed and comfortable. We awakened to a good breakfast and went back to the theater for the second day. We were certainly unprepared for what happened.

Chapter 5

IT PROMISED TO BE A very busy Sunday. Not only was I scheduled to hold almost forty more auditions, but there was to be a working lunch as well. I looked forward to conferring with the designers at noon.

Well, not really *all* the designers. Lighting, sound and costumes were to be handled by people I had never met. I had been told that these three were regulars at the Barn Theater and worked on every show the theater produced. They apparently had day jobs elsewhere and performed their important duties at the theater "just for fun." Lord, please deliver me from fun-loving amateurs.

The morning auditions had not been particularly successful, so my mood had soured a bit when Sophie and I had our first meeting with these techies. A word or two about each will suffice I believe to paint an accurate picture of my new colleagues.

Upon entering the green room, I was at once athletically bear hugged by the massive, tattooed biceps of the lighting designer, Joey Patowski. "Joey" is short for Johanna who, I learned, normally assists home remodeling customers with all their electrical and plumbing needs at the local Home Depot. She was a friendly, outgoing, muscular gal who reminded me of a giant but scraggly Newfoundland dog, not unlike Nana in "Peter Pan." When I whispered this observation to Sophie, she almost choked on her liverwurst sandwich. I suspected from my brief discussion of the plays' lighting needs with Joey that I could expect her to provide the appropriate hardware. But I feared that the subtleties of mood and atmosphere which theatrical lighting could so magically provide were not within her ken.

Ken, incidentally, was the first name of the sound designer who, it happened, was a CPA by trade. A spindly, graying man who physically matched perfectly the controlled, unemotional stereotype of his profession, Ken's passion it seemed was not for number crunching but, rather, for audio. He lived for stereo components, mixers, amplifiers, coaxial speakers, tweeters, woofers, subwoofers and a million other pieces of equipment. Although normally quite laconic, should the subject turn in the direction of his interest, he would gladly drone on endlessly in an especially irritating adenoidal monotone. Ken Gleason was by day a quiet, unassuming, button-downed accountant; by night he was a wonky wizard of sound reproduction and recording. After looking at him and listening to him, one could be excused for thinking that sound reproduction was the only type at which he was expert. When I made this *sub rosa* comment to Sophie, she almost coughed up her Waldorf salad.

Sylvie Darnell's high spirited energy and inextinguishable ebullience were in marked contrast to Ken's low-keyed self-control or Joey's blue denimed good nature. This fashion maven was dressed in the brightest, trendiest designer labels adorned with enough feathers and frills, froufrous and googas to choke a giant Newfoundland. I feared her views on costume design would be in marked contrast to mine, so I braced myself for the worst and asked her to bring to our next meeting wardrobe sketches for each character appropriately swatched. We shall see what Sylvie comes up with. I came up with a wry comment to make about this diva fashionista, but with a look Sophie prevented me from revealing it to her, protesting that she was wearing a new blouse and didn't want to spill the red wine she was sipping all over it. She also quietly admonished me to "act my age and learn to play nice with the new kids."

Of course she was right. I can only blame my juvenile rudeness on the fact that I was impatient to talk with Charlie Wetherstone. A month ago, when the selection committee of the board advised me that I had been selected, I was asked to recommend a capable person to double as the theater's technical director and set designer. Apparently their longtime T.D. had recently lost his life in a tragic traffic accident. I gave them Charlie's name and was delighted to hear a few days later that he had been hired.

I had always liked Charlie Wetherstone. We had first met when we were students at Yale. A very talented set designer and master of all tools, Charlie was basically a very sweet and decent young man but unfortunately had been his own worst enemy. Although most members of our class had been relatively wild, including myself, I am afraid that pot and booze quickly became Charlie's closest companions, and after some sort of scandal involving underage young ladies he was asked to leave the program at the end of the first year.

From time to time over the years we ran into each other. He always was very complimentary about my work and growing success. His career had not been as fortunate. He worked now and then in regional theater, but the rumor mill insinuated that he had not yet licked his demons. A number of years ago, I received a lovely note from him after I had pulled a few strings to wangle him a national tour. The note was accompanied by a photo of him and his new puppy, a black lab/pit bull mix named Lucy. Both Charlie and Lucy looked healthy and happy in the snapshot posed somewhere along the Oregon coastline. I remember that he had been kind enough to thank me for the upward turn his life had taken and looked forward to introducing me to Miss Lucy, "the only female I've ever really understood." A few years after that my schedule allowed me to run into him in Chicago where we spent a very pleasant evening. I noticed that he restricted himself to club sodas that evening. His devotion to the dog and hers to him were quite remarkable and rather touching. I was pleased old Charlie had straightened out his life. Sophie had kept in touch with him over the years as well, and it was she who had provided me with his current address last month to give to the board.

I had discussed the basic technical requirements of the shows with him in a few friendly and engaging email messages last week. The theater had found a little house right outside Brookfield for him to rent at a reasonable rate this summer, and he and Lucy (now a matron of seven) were to arrive in town sometime yesterday. With all the chaos going on yesterday I had not had a chance to see or speak with Charlie. I therefore was looking forward to our getting reacquainted face to face at this meeting and working together on this challenging project over the summer.

But where was he? Lunch had been devoured, my basic introductions to the other designers had been accomplished, small talk was diminishing and still no Charlie.

Sophie called his cell phone number. I was astonished that somehow her phone managed to get a signal but was disappointed when she only reached his voice mail. Leaving a message for him to call either of us as soon as he could, Sophie and I bid adieu to the three members of the production team who had shown up, and after another hearty hug from Joey, a grunt and a tepid handshake from Ken and six air kisses from Sylvie, we returned to the afternoon auditions.

Throughout the afternoon, Sophie kept trying to reach Charlie but to no avail. One phone call did come in, but it was Belinda asking if I'd like to meet her after the auditions for a little dinner. I would have liked to have conversed with her at greater length, but the beady eyes of Buster McGraw were drilling into me impatiently waiting to begin his monologue. So I merely said I'd love to meet her and made plans to do so at the hospital at seven, as she would soon be on her way there. By the by, Buster's Brutus was a bomb.

As were the majority of the second day's auditions. The afternoon session was therefore a little shorter because of this. It was only a bit after 5:30 that I handed Sophie the list now marked with the additional six callback names. I was a little snotty when I pointed out to her that she had only starred four of today's six superior actors. "I'm afraid you're losing your touch, old thing." I smirked. Somehow Sophie didn't seem a bit fazed but instead handed me a piece of paper.

"Since we haven't heard from Charlie, I asked the theater for the address of the house he's renting. What say we go out there and see if he's arrived yet?" Sophie seemed a bit concerned, and since I had some time to spare before I was to meet Belinda I agreed.

My rental car had come equipped with a GPS device, so we decided to go in my car to find our way more easily "over the river and through the woods," since the pastures and trees surrounding the theater all looked pretty much the same to me, and my sense of direction had never been very reliable. I had already posted the address of Pemberley Cottage as my home base on this clever little machine and now punched in Brookfield Memorial Hospital and 17 Upper Creek Road (Charlie's address) to add to the Barn Theater as favorite destinations. It should be a snap finding my way around these unfamiliar surroundings.

Unfamiliar yes, but I must say they were very, very pleasant to drive through. For some reason I now viewed the scenery much more appreciatively than I had yesterday. The late afternoon sun filtering through the branches of the fruit trees bathed the fields and farmhouses with a soft glow. It was impossible to feel anything but hopeful on a day like this. Even for cynical, glass-half-empty me. Yes, hopeful. Hopeful that my life, like Charlie's, was now on a major upswing. Despite the modicum of fame I had achieved and the promise that my new works would lead to even more, I had felt for some time (I blush to admit it) that there was something missing. Despite the rather large number of attractive, and I must say, extremely affectionate lady friends I've had over the years, I had never considered selecting just one and settling down. Never once that is until last evening. I was startled to realize that I was tremendously looking forward to renewing old times and moving on to newer, even better ones with Charlie and in a different, more profound way with Belinda.

I was barely aware that we had managed to navigate the myriad country twists and turns and unmarked lanes and had arrived at the property Charlie was to rent until I heard, "You have reached your destination." The no nonsense, Mid-Atlantic tones of "Mandy," the anthropomorphic name given to our ethereal GPS-directing tour guide, awoke me from my reverie. We parked in front of the metal rural mail box. I noted that the red flag was raised. According to Sophie this indicated that mail was waiting to be picked up. Although the outline of the tiny bungalow could barely be perceived at the top of the gradually inclining hill about one hundred yards before us, what I could see of the house and its surrounding acreage struck me as the perfect spot for initiating a joyous new beginning. I knew Charlie would love it here. "Perhaps Belinda and I..." My fantasy was interrupted by the faint sounds of what appeared to be a dog frantically barking.

CHAPTER

6

CHARLES WETHERSTONE HAD NOT APPEARED at the production meeting, nor had he returned our phone messages. Therefore in the late afternoon on Sunday my assistant and I drove to the house he had contracted to rent for the summer to try to locate him. We were successful.

"That must be Lucy warning Charlie of our arrival," I cried out with a sense of relief. "That son of a b must be here after all. Why didn't that bastard show up at the meeting? Is he so full of himself these days that he couldn't at least have the common courtesy to return our calls? He better have a twenty-four carat jewel encrusted iron clad excuse, or he damn well will get a piece of my mind!"

Sophie smiled at me, "I know, Harry. I was worried too." Turning to her, I shyly returned the smile. It was a lovely moment between us. Have I mentioned before how glad I was Sophie was in my life?

As she started walking up the dirt path, I took my time following her, savoring the beauty all around me. I think it was the sweetness of honeysuckle that bewitched my nasal membranes. I think it was the scarlet flash of a pair of cardinals that delighted my eye as they were startled into flight by the distant barking. I think it was the jaunty

Halloween colors of a Monarch butterfly leisurely enjoying the nectar of a wild rose that made my breath catch in my throat. I knew I was behaving like an idiot when I began softly singing, "In our mountain greenery/ Where God paints the scenery," but I didn't for the life of me care. I was just getting to "Let blue skies be your coverlet" when the sound of a sharp intake of breath interrupted my impromptu Rodgers and Hart concert.

Sophie had opened the front door of what was apparently Charlie's old van parked about ten yards to the left and had poked her nose inside. The troubled look on her face brought me suddenly back to reality.

"What's wrong, Sophie?"

She didn't respond but instead started running up the path at a remarkably rapid clip. I didn't take the time to look inside the van but instead, huffing and puffing, tried to shorten the distance between us. The hill was considerably steeper now as we finally got a better view of the bungalow about twenty yards ahead of us. I could see Lucy's head inside the house at one of the front windows. She spotted us and then manically careened back and forth among all four of the windows. Her incessant barking grew louder and more unnerving as we got closer to the tiny front porch. Still a few yards ahead of me, Sophie leaped up the three stairs in one bound and tried the front door. It was unlocked. She quickly entered.

I almost jumped out of my skin as Lucy immediately shot out of the house, quickly relieved herself and then, howling wildly in a way I shall never forget, sprinted around the back and out of sight.

I didn't know what to do. Should I go in the house after Sophie? Should I follow Lucy? Foolishly but insistently the question, "Where's Timmy, Lassie?" stuck in my brain.

"Harry," Sophie's voice was quiet and strained as she stood on the porch, "look in here."

I can't remember ever walking as slowly as I did as I forced myself to enter the dimly lit interior of the small bungalow. The smell of liquor hit me like a sledgehammer as soon as I walked into the front room. "My God, it smells like a brewery in here," my voice sounded bewildered and horrified and angry all at the same time.

"I know. His car smelled the same." I almost missed Sophie's soft declarative sentence because my heart was thumping so loudly.

There was a crunching sound as I stepped forward. Looking down I saw broken glass everywhere. What looked like smashed liquor bottles littered the floor. An opened suitcase leaned precariously over an armchair with half of its contents crumpled and trod upon. Lucy's food and water bowls were empty and stood forlornly in the kitchen. The faucet was slowly dripping. When Sophie turned the handle, the sudden silence was unsettling. The door leading to what must be the bedroom was half ajar. Sophie and I looked at each other for several seconds, and then with a feeling of dread I slowly pushed the door fully open and walked into the bedroom.

My heart stopped as I stared at the bulky shape on the bed. But no, thank God, it was not what my horrified eyes had taken for a decapitated body. It was only a large, heavily filled duffle bag lying across the blanket-covered bed. Another empty bottle lay beside the bag. I breathed once again and rejoined Sophie. "He's not in there."

"The bathroom is empty too," she softly reported. It seemed appropriate for both of us to be whispering.

What could have happened to Charlie to make him go on such a binge? And where was he now? These unspoken questions were obviously on both our minds as we stepped back outside. After the murkiness of the bungalow, the sunlight was disconcerting and strangely incongruous.

We both jumped as the unearthly cries of Lucy's howling sliced the air. We quickly scooted around to the back of the house and began to follow the sounds. The house stood at the crest of the hill. The land in back leveled off for a bit and then began to descend. It became more heavily wooded as we continued moving as quickly as we could. The dog's fierce howling had now changed to a harrowing low wail that tore at my guts. At Sophie's too. "Oh, God, Harry, what's happening? Where is he? Lucy! Loooceeeee!"

Frantically calling out the dog's name, Sophie rushed forward through a thick grove of trees and almost lost her balance as the land suddenly took a sharp decline. When I caught up with her, she was looking down, her hands covering a silent scream.

When we discovered the body, we called Dr. Freemount. He in turn called 911. We waited for them to arrive.

No matter how hard I try, I don't think I'll ever be able to forget that sight. The thickly layered brush steeply descended to the bank of the slowly moving creek below us. The soft gurgling of the water formed an eerie background to Lucy's moaning and whimpering. The light shining on her back caused her dark fur to glow with a strangely mystical copper colored sheen. She was lying down on the edge of the bank leaning over something. Although we climbed down as quickly as we could, it was difficult not to stumble over the rough terrain, and several times we caught ourselves from falling. Finally we reached the tangled bank and saw that Lucy was licking his left hand.

We could only see the very top of Charlie's head. His face, right arm and shoulder were submerged in the shallow water. He was lying perpendicular to the creek, and his left arm lay on the ground beside the rest of his body in a strangely relaxed posture.

There was no question in our minds that he was gone and had been so for some time.

And yet everything seemed so normal. The water in the creek flowed pleasantly. The mild breeze stirred the bulrushes on the edge of the water languorously. Softly buzzing insects enjoyed their aerial acrobatics above the scene totally unconcerned that a good man had lost his life and that his loyal and devoted friend was desperately laboring beside him. Desperately trying to bring her master back to life with her tongue. A ray of sunlight capriciously fell on the broken bottle lying a foot or so away from the body causing the glass to shine blazingly in our tear-stained eyes.

It was Sophie who sensibly advised me not to touch the body. It was Sophie who sensibly called Augie Freemount on her cell phone. It was Sophie who sensibly tried to move Lucy away from her task. But in this last action Sophie failed. The dog would not be moved nor could be dissuaded to cease her whimpering. Occasionally, she turned to us with a questioning, grief-filled expression in her brown eyes. But we could do nothing to help her; we could do nothing to help him. So Lucy returned to his hand and continued the only thing she could do. And so we waited.

It took Augie less than fifteen minutes to get there. Another five or ten minutes and the ambulance and police arrived. I assume they all performed their functions in a considerate and professional manner. I assume they were considerate and professional to Sophie and me by limiting their questions to the barest essentials. I assume they were as considerate and professional as possible when they finally were able to carry the dog away and put her in the police car. I assume they were as considerate and professional as possible when they removed the body from its resting place, covered it with a blanket and carried it into the waiting ambulance. I can only assume these things because I was only vaguely aware of what was happening. I was only vaguely aware when Sophie took me by the arm and helped me into our car. I was only vaguely aware of Sophie driving us to the hospital following the ambulance and police car. I vaguely remembered asking Sophie why they bothered blaring the siren. I vaguely remembered asking Sophie "Where's Timmy?" before beginning to sob.

CHAPTER

7

"HOW COULD THIS HAVE HAPPENED?" "How could this have happened?" Like a mantra, I repeated this question over and over during the next several hours. I asked it of Sophie who was as perplexed as I while we sat in the hospital waiting room. I asked it of Belinda when she so kindly joined us there while we waited for the medical findings. I asked it of Dr. Freemount after he so patiently explained to us the reasons why he listed the official cause of death as an unfortunate accident. I asked it of the detectives after they had so carefully and logically reiterated to us why their conclusions matched those of the doctor's. They all agreed that Charlie had been heavily drinking (his blood alcohol level was sky high). He had wandered out of the house in a drunken stupor. He had lost his footing and fallen down the embankment. He had hit his forehead sharply on a rock as he fell face down in the creek. And he had drowned in a foot of water. Forensics (whatever the hell they were) and extensive medical examinations and tests had all established this as fact to everyone's complete satisfaction.

Everyone's but mine! Sometime, somehow during these hours of watching and listening to sympathetic lips providing sympathetic smiles and sympathetic explanations, the mantra inside my brain had changed from "How could this have happened?" to "It couldn't have happened this way."

I had no evidence to support this. I just knew it. I knew that Charlie had turned his life around. I knew that Charlie had succeeded in quitting drinking. I knew that the Charlie who had emailed me such positive, upbeat, funny, relaxed and self confident messages only last week could never have reverted to such self-destructive behavior.

I just knew it. Now I had to prove it.

Belinda was of course very understanding when I requested a rain check for dinner. She also eased my mind a bit about Lucy. During the time Sophie and I had been talking with the police, Belinda had gone back up to her brother's room. Since Robert was an active volunteer with the local animal rescue shelter, Belinda had asked him to check on Lucy's condition. Robert immediately called a friend at the shelter who assured him that Lucy was being well taken care of there. Since Robert was due to be discharged from the hospital tomorrow, he also promised to visit Lucy himself on Monday and advise us how she was doing.

After one last goodbye to Belinda and Augie, Sophie and I left the hospital and got back into the car. "I don't remember ever being so bushed," Sophie sighed as she turned on the GPS. "Let's go back to the theater so I can pick up my car, and then we can both try to get a good night's sleep at the Freemounts."

"I have a different idea," I said stopping her finger from clicking "Pemberley Cottage" as our destination.

Sophie gave me a quizzical look when she saw that I had chosen Charlie's address instead. "What's up, boss? I noticed some weird change in your behavior the last hour or so. Weirder than usual, that is."

When I didn't react to her dig, Sophie grew quiet and more serious. "Come on, give."

She listened quietly as I told her what I felt, what I knew, even though

I had no proof of any kind to back me up. When I had finished, we sat in silence for a few moments.

"So what are you saying, Harry? If it wasn't a terrible accident caused by Charlie drinking again, then what was it?"

"I can't even begin to speculate. I only know I'll never rest until I find out the truth. So I'm going back to Charlie's house to see what I can find. And I'd very much like you to go with me. What do you say?"

"Well … it wouldn't be the first wild goose chase we've taken together. And I'm sure it won't be the last. Lead on, Macduff."

"Actually the line is '*Lay* on Macduff,' but who's quibbling?" I gratefully replied.

Muttering "You scum bag" under her breath, Sophie let *Mandy* lead us on through the darkening woods and country roads till we parked once again by the metal mail box.

For a time, neither of us moved or said a word. We just sat there in the front seat seemingly watching the shadows lengthening and listening to the restful, hypnotic sounds of dusk. But mostly, I think, we were trying to reconcile the gentle peacefulness of the here and now with the chaotic confusion that took place here just a few hours ago.

Finally, Sophie broke the spell. "It's not too late for us to change our minds, you know."

This got me going. "No, Sophie, we owe it to Charlie to look around at least a little. And we'll start right here."

The harsh sound of the car door slamming behind me startled us both as I got out and, noticing that the red flag was still standing vertically, opened the mailbox. It contained two stamped envelopes. As the daylight was fading, I opened the car door next to Sophie and let out a surprised cry. The light of the car's interior illuminated my own name neatly printed on the face of the first envelope.

The envelope which was the size that normally held greeting cards was addressed to: Mr. Harrison Hunt in care of the Brookfield Inn, 168 Tremont Street, Brookfield. The return address read: Charles W. Wetherstone, 17 Upper Creek Road, Brookfield.

"You'll never believe this, Sophie. I think Charlie was sending *me* a card."

"Are you kidding?" Sophie exclaimed.

"In fact, he also was sending one to *you*," I said handing her the other envelope which was addressed to her also in care of the Inn.

"Holey, moley, speaking of weird," she shuddered, "This is really beginning to creep me out. It's certainly not my birthday. What do you think they say? And why would Charlie be mailing us cards when he was supposed to be seeing us in person today?"

"There's only one way of finding out," I said as I started to open my envelope.

"Wait a sec, Harry. Isn't it a federal offense or something to interfere with the U.S. mail?"

"They're addressed to *us*, Sophie."

"Oh, right. But should we be tampering with possible evidence involved in a criminal case?"

"The official consensus seems to be that no crime has taken place. I say we take a look at what Charlie wanted to say to us." And before Sophie could offer any further objection, I ripped open the top of the envelope.

But before I got to remove the contents, Sophie sensibly stated, "Okay, but let's hold off reading them until we get to a place that's a little more private. And if you want to look for any more 'clues' outdoors, Mr. Holmes, I suggest we do so now, before it gets completely dark. We can read the cards to our hearts' content when we reach the house."

Agreeing with her logic, I put the envelopes in my jacket pocket.

Before she left the car, Sophie reached into her ever present tote bag of tricks and came up with two penlights, one of which she handed to me.

"Here, hold on to one of these, in case we might need them later."

We slowly began our walk up the dirt path. Looking carefully at the ground for anything out of the ordinary, we came up empty handed until we reached Charlie's van. This was the first time I had looked inside. The van still reeked of liquor. I noticed that an empty scotch bottle was lying on the back seat.

Sophie dutifully entered this item and everything else we found on the small notepad she was carrying.

Front and back seats:

1 empty bottle scotch whiskey
4 paper bags containing empty fast food containers
2 empty bottles bottled water
1 printout Google Maps itinerary
1 umbrella with 2 broken spokes
2 copies HH's scripts

Glove compartment:

Van's registration papers
Van's insurance policy
1 pair sunglasses
1 pair spectacles
Several receipts & other scraps paper
1 opened bottle antacid pills
1 opened bottle aspirins
1 digital camera
1 tube sunscreen

I put the camera and all the pieces of paper in my other jacket pockets to be examined in more detail later.

We could see the bungalow looming in front of us. It was really getting quite dark now, so we both took out our flashlights to better look at the ground in front of the house when we almost jumped out of our skins.

Astonishingly, music suddenly erupted from the unlit house in front of us. Bouncy digitized saxophones and bongos.

Da da da da/ Dadaah da da/

Da da da da/ Dadaah da da/

"What the hell is that?" Sophie shrieked.

"Can't you tell? It's the theme song from *I Love Lucy*."

CHAPTER
8

IT TOOK ME A FEW seconds to realize that the music issuing from the house must be the ringtone of Charlie's cell phone. What better choice could he have made than the theme from this classic sitcom? I wondered if he had named his dog after the beloved redhead.

We both raced up the last few yards of the path and up the front steps as fast as we could. But the need to light the way with the flashlights slowed us down a bit. I pushed open the front door a moment after the music had suddenly and abruptly ceased.

Frustrated that I had missed the call, I was equally frustrated in trying to find the light switch, as it was now pitch black in the house. Even with Sophie shining her penlight over the walls, I still managed to bump my knee painfully twice before I finally was able to flip on the light in the front room.

My irritation at Sophie's lack of appropriate sympathy at my discomfort faded as my eyes adjusted to the sudden change of brightness. In the stark glare of the ceiling fixture, the room looked even bleaker and more somber than it had this afternoon. I was feeling more and more the way Sophie had put it a few minutes ago: really creeped out.

But back to business. Where was that cell phone? We spent several minutes searching for it in vain, until Sophie had the good sense of using her own phone to call Charlie's. The *Lucy* theme brightly started up again, and we were successful in locating the phone near the duffle bag in the bedroom.

Since Sophie was familiar with the operating procedures of Charlie's phone model, she activated its voice mail and speaker phone. Sitting down at the small table in the front room, we listened as the automated voice reported that there were eight new messages.

"Eight," I exclaimed. "How long has it been since he checked them?"

Of course the first seven turned out to be Sophie's attempts to reach Charlie during the afternoon auditions. We both grew impatient as we were forced to listen to Sophie's voice over and over again. Finally, the eighth and final message, the one presumably we had just missed, came on loud and clear. We heard a man's hearty, baritone voice. It was a voice neither one of us recognized.

"*Hey, Meathead! It's me. How's it hanging, guy? Boy was I thrilled to get the invite and I'll be RSVPing right away. But I'm calling to let you know just how proud I am of you and how pleased as punch I am that you two are going through with this. Nobody knows better than I how much you've had to struggle over the years and how worrying this latest thing has been for you. But you and I both know how much you've accomplished, and I'm so happy that you two have made the decision to plow ahead no matter what. We'll find out who's doing this, and we'll triumph over it. Just as we've triumphed over everything else. You're some terrific guy, Charlie. And you know I'm behind you and Hazel one hundred percent. Congratulations again, and call me at home when you get this message. I'm so proud of you, kid, and so damned happy. Take care.*"

At the prompt, Sophie chose to save the message, and after we were told that there were no additional new messages, we sat at the table silently trying to make sense of what we had heard.

Finally, Sophie said, "Well, I bet we can guess what's inside those mysterious envelopes Charlie was sending us. Let's open them."

Nodding, I removed them from my jacket pocket and giving hers to Sophie opened the one addressed to me. As anticipated, they were formally engraved wedding invitations. We carefully read over every word several times.

We invite you to join us
in celebrating our love.
On this day we shall marry the person
we laugh with, live for, dream with.
We have chosen to continue our growth
through marriage.

Please join
Hazel Elizabeth Forrest
&
Charles Henry Wetherstone

Saturday, the eighteenth of October
at three o'clock in the afternoon
Portland Community Center
Portland, Oregon
Feast and Merriment to follow

Please R.S.V.P. at our wedding website:
www.walkdowntheaisle.com/Forrest Wetherstone

I didn't remember ever having seen Sophie weep before. I didn't know where to look as she sat silently in her wooden chair with tears streaming down her face.

I didn't cry. Instead, I became angry. Charlie's friends owed it to his memory to find out the truth. Whoever the caller was who had left the message, he certainly respected Charlie for the courage he had shown in changing his life and wholeheartedly believed that only good things lay in his future. If Charlie had indeed gone on a drunken rampage that had resulted in his death, something or someone horrendous must have precipitated it. I was determined to uncover this something or someone.

"Poor, dear Charlie," Sophie said softly, "and that poor, poor girl."

"Let's help both of them by finding out what really happened. What did the fellow on the phone mean by saying he knew how worrying *this latest thing* has been for Charlie? What latest thing? And he said they'll find out *who's doing this*. Doing what? When we find out what Charlie's friend meant, we'll be in a better position to help."

"You know I'm with you all the way, Harry," she said wiping her eyes. "Now, if I remember correctly, the guy on the phone didn't leave his name. But Charlie's cell phone should have a record of the caller's number. Let me check on that now." She quickly went about her task.

"Oh, that's just great." Sophie's exasperated response a moment later indicated that she hadn't obtained what she had expected. "The caller's phone number is listed as restricted. So, I think that unless we get some special help from the phone company, we won't be able to get his number."

"Well, we probably won't have to go to that trouble," I said. "We should be able to get it from Hazel Forrest, I would think, when we reach her."

"Right, and I would think we can find her phone number right here in Charlie's cell phone directory. Now, let's see. Yes, here it is. Should we call her now?"

"Let's wait a bit on that. I don't think I'm up to delivering the news of Charlie's death to his fiancée right this minute. Maybe we should give her number to the police anyway. Aren't they supposed to contact the next of kin and the like?"

"I guess you're right."

"You know, Sophie. I'm still pretty astonished to learn that Charlie was engaged. I didn't even know that he was seeing anyone special. Did you?"

"Not a clue. Mind you I only checked in with him every few months or so and then only a quick email. And he always kept personal things pretty close to the vest."

"Right, that was my impression too."

There was a pause and then Sophie suddenly stood up and began rapidly speaking. "Oh, Harry, I want to get out of this place. I keep expecting Charlie to open the front door and tell us it was all a joke." She started to laugh. "You know what a practical joker he was. I keep expecting him and Lucy to run in and ..."

I took her in my arms and held her while she sobbed for a minute or two. She slowly recovered and sheepishly said, "Thanks, boss. My word, what an old softie I seem to have turned into." She interrupted me from speaking. "No, that's quite enough mush for now. Our job is to find out what happened to that poor guy. So let's get moving and see what we can discover in the house. I'll look through the bedroom and bathroom and you take the front room and kitchen area. Okay?"

I smiled at her, and we began our search. As we had noticed this afternoon, Charlie's opened suitcase was perched half on and half off an armchair and some of its contents had fallen out on the floor. But I found nothing but clothes (some of them clearly had been walked upon) and his toiletry kit in and around the suitcase. Sophie emptied the duffle bag in the bedroom but only found more clothing (work clothes), shoes, tools and preparatory work Charlie had done for the show. Sophie added what we had found to her notebook.

Interior of House

1 cell phone

1 suitcase: shirts, dress pants, sport jacket, 1 pair dress shoes, 1 pair sneakers, underwear, socks, belt, tie, bathing suit

1 duffle bag: work shirts, work pants, jacket, set of wrenches, 6 technical drawings of sets, 2 cardboard models of sets, drafting tools, 2 paperback books

2 plastic dog bowls

1 bag dog food (unopened)

1 bottle scotch whiskey (empty)

Broken pieces of whiskey bottle on floor

That seemed to be everything. So what had happened? It certainly appeared that when Charlie had first entered the house, he had dropped his suitcase on the armchair, dropped his duffle bag on the bed, put down the food and water bowls for Lucy, opened the suitcase, and then had done nothing else but drink. Nothing had been unpacked. Nothing had been put in the closet or bureau or bathroom. There was no evidence of food or water residue in Lucy's bowls. It looked like the only thing on Charlie's mind when he came into the house was to continue the drinking he had started in the van.

Dispirited, we sat down once again at the table. There must be something else we had missed. There must be something. I looked at Sophie's notebook one more time. Suddenly it hit me.

CHAPTER 9

WHERE WAS CHARLIE'S LAPTOP? AS far as I knew, he always had it with him. Especially when he was on the road. Sophie was always able to reach him by email whenever she tried to contact him. He and I had communicated via email only last week. I believe he had even then been on the road en route to Brookfield by way of several stops along the way. But we had seen no sign of his computer either in the van or in the bungalow. So what had happened to it? If it had been damaged during his supposed drunken frenzy, there still should be pieces of it in the house. But we had found neither hide nor hair of it.

When I brought this up to Sophie, she was as mystified as I.

"Could he have taken it with him when he left the house and fell down the embankment?" she halfheartedly suggested.

I said it didn't sound particularly plausible but we could go outside now and look again, even though we hadn't seen any sign of a laptop when we had followed Lucy's trail to the creek this afternoon.

Sophie thought better of that idea. "I really think it would be safer for us to do more exploring in that rough terrain only in the daylight. There've been enough catastrophes today for my taste, thank you very much."

Truthfully, I was relieved she felt this way. So, taking with us Charlie's cell phone as well as his drawings and models (they would be a boon to whoever would be building the set), we left the house. As we hadn't yet looked carefully at the front porch, we did so now. My flashlight revealed nothing of interest, and I had descended the steps and was on the path when I heard Sophie call out.

Looking back, I could see her flashlight shining on something on the edge of the top step. When I rejoined her, I saw that she had picked up a yellow piece of paper. It was a notice that the UPS had tried to deliver a package. But since there had been no one at home to sign for it, the package would be returned to their office and be available for pickup on Monday morning at 9:00 am. The notice was dated yesterday and was addressed to C. Wetherstone. We assumed that the notice had been inserted in the doorframe but had fallen off somehow and been caught in a crack in the top step. We most assuredly would be visiting the UPS office bright and early the next morning.

Putting the notice in my pocket along with the other pieces of paper already there, we returned to the car without further adventure.

Inside the car Sophie said, "I don't know about you, but I'm ready for a home-cooked meal and a stiff drink."

"I can't think of anything more appealing, but it's almost 9:00, too late to beg a meal from the Freemounts, I'm afraid."

"Maybe not," she said. "When I called Louise Freemount from the hospital to tell her we didn't know when we'd be back and not to hold dinner for us, she said not to worry. She was used to putting together meals at the last minute because of her husband's erratic schedule. So, Harry, why don't you give her a call now and see? While you're doing that, I'll phone the sixteen actors and Belinda to work out the times for their callbacks Tuesday evening."

Without further ado, she reached into her tote bag, retrieved the casting sheets and her cell phone and started making her calls. Knowing how temperamental my damned phone was, I expected more aggravation. But lo and behold, it instantly sprang to life, and Louise answered on the second ring. She was graciousness incarnate saying she'd see us shortly for dinner and would beef tenderloin be to our liking. I told her I was practically salivating at the thought. Hearing Louise's voice for the first time on the phone triggered some long inactive synapse in my brain. She certainly reminded me of someone, but for the life of me I couldn't remember who.

Having the luxury of Mandy to guide us through the bewildering twists and turns of Brookfield's byways freed us from having to think much about directions and allowed us the time to rehash the day's events and make our plans for the next couple of days. Sophie wrote down the main points once again in her ever ready notebook.

The theater

1. Callbacks now all scheduled for Tuesday from 6 – 8 pm at theater. Final readings and casting decisions to be made beginning at 8pm
2. 6 weeks of rehearsals to begin Wednesday
3. Need to find new TD and Set Designer to replace CW (discuss with AF &/or other boardmembers tonite?)

The mystery of CW's death

1. Need to review carefully all pieces of paper collected from CW's van
2. Need to decide whether to call fiancée (HF) or ask police to contact her
3. Need contact info from HF about CW's friend with restricted phone #
4. Need info from him about allusions made in his phone message
5. Need to go to UPS office Monday 9am to pick up package (refer to yellow UPS notice)

6. Need to receive RG's info about welfare of Lucy after he visits Shelter Monday

7. Try to locate CW's laptop (explore land behind house all way to creek?)

As we were pulling into the driveway of Pemberley Cottage, Sophie had just jotted down the next item we had come up with:

8. Need to investigate all #s on CW's cell phone directory

As we parked the car, Sophie interjected another interesting thought. "Wouldn't it be useful to know as much as we can of Charlie's whereabouts and actions once he arrived in Brookfield? And maybe even the details of his entire car trip here from Portland? That's where the Google Maps printout we found in the van started, I believe."

"Your logical mind and organizational skills will surely be a godsend here," I gibed.

"And all this time you've thought I was just compulsively anal," she laughed.

"And who says I've changed my opinion?"

There were a number of *sotto voce* mutterings coming out of Sophie's mouth as we walked up the front steps of Pemberley Cottage. I thought better of asking her to repeat them.

It was Augie Freemount who answered the door and welcomingly ushered us into the charming sitting room. He told us Louise would join us shortly as she was finishing the preparations for dinner in the kitchen. As he poured out our eagerly anticipated cocktails, he remarked that we must be looking forward to turning in early tonight. "I'm sure you both must be as exhausted as I am."

"I hope your days aren't always as stressful as the past two have been," Sophie commiserated.

"Thankfully not," the doctor said. "It's usually pretty quiet around here. There's been more excitement since you two have arrived than this little town has seen in a long time. Especially today. What a horrible way for your friend to pass. Such a tragedy. I've seen a number of equally sad outcomes tied to alcohol abuse over the years, and each one was so terrible because it could have been averted, it should have been prevented. And it's always so especially hard on the loved ones."

"Charlie had a fiancée," I said.

"I know," Augie replied. "I just got through talking to Miss Forrest."

"You did?" Sophie and I sat up startled.

"Yup. Mr. Wetherstone had listed her as his emergency contact on the employment forms he filled out for the theater. I called Bitsie Adams, who handles all the theater's paperwork, and got her phone number. I spoke to her soon after you two left the hospital. Lovely girl. Do you know her well?"

"I'm afraid not."

"She was shocked of course when I told her of the accident. And it took a few minutes for it to register on her that he was dead. But when it did, she seemed to become quite calm. I told her we'd leave all his possessions here until she arrives."

"Hazel Forrest is coming here?" Sophie asked.

"Oh yes, she'll be flying in tomorrow and will take the body back to Oregon for burial."

Before either of us could react to this news, a loud crash sounded somewhere in the house followed immediately by a high-pitched scream. Augie quickly ran in the direction of the sounds. Without thinking, Sophie and I followed him.

When we entered the large, brightly lit kitchen, we saw Augie kneeling on the floor. Cradled in his arms was his wife Louise groaning.

CHAPTER 10

AUGIE AND LOUISE CALLED US into the dining room where we sat down to the elegant meal Louise had prepared. It was almost as if the last fifteen minutes had never occurred.

As soon as we had entered the kitchen in a panic, Augie had calmly told us it was nothing to worry about and asked me to return to the sitting room and Sophie to fetch his medical bag and first aid kit which he kept in the hall closet. We did as we were told and, after performing her errand, Sophie rejoined me on the settee.

We waited as instructed wondering if Louise would indeed be all right as Augie had told Sophie she would be. We could hear the Freemounts speaking quietly to each other but could not make out any words. It looked as if the pot of soup Louise had dropped had scalded her a bit on the hand, and Sophie had seen Augie take out a tube of salve and a roll of bandage before she was asked to leave him alone to "take care of this little matter," as he had put it.

"I assume this was just another *accident*," Sophie whispered to me stressing the last word, "but how many of them have to take place before you just have to have doubts. That makes three people who have collapsed or fallen in our vicinity in the past two days. Sure, Robert

PAUL EISEMAN

Gregory seems to have recovered and Louise apparently is not seriously injured, but Charlie is dead from a so-called *accident*, and God knows what's going to happen next. This is the screwiest place I've ever seen, and I wouldn't mind it in the least if we got the bejeezus out of here."

I put my arm around Sophie and gave her shoulder a reassuring squeeze. "I'm as confused and angry as you are, Sophie, but let's try to hang in there and find out what indeed is going on. I think if we carefully and logically follow all the steps you've itemized so cogently we'll be able to discover a solution to this *rural riddle*."

Sophie looked up at me and saw in my eyes what I was trying to do. "Oh, alliteration will get you anywhere, Lord Byron. How about *pastoral puzzle?*" she grinned.

"Or *country conundrum?*" I continued.

"Or *suburban stumper?*" she giggled.

I was about to add *bucolic brainteaser* but was interrupted by Augie's entrance. He looked a bit pale but seemed pretty calm and collected. "Louise is so embarrassed by all of this. Please excuse us if we added more angst to your terrible day."

"Don't be silly," I said. "How's she doing?"

"She's fine. Just a minor burn. She's gone upstairs to put on a new face, *her* expression not mine I assure you. I'm delighted with the old one."

"As you surely should be. Your wife is a lovely woman."

There was a wistful expression in Augie's eyes as he said, "Thank you. Yes she is. She, in fact, is the love of my life."

The pause that followed was a little awkward, and we were both thinking of a way to fill it when Louise came in ringing a little silver bell. "I would have said 'Soup's On,'" she laughed, "if I hadn't so clumsily spilled it all. But we'll make do anyway."

We more than made do. The dinner (even without the soup) was delicious. Louise's bandaged hand in no way impeded the serving of each delectable course, and it was pleasant to see how Augie lovingly helped her with both the serving and clearing. All in all, the delightful meal and company helped Sophie and me to unwind.

Much more relaxed, I felt quite comfortable talking with both Augie and Louise. The need to find a new technical director/set designer was discussed. Since we had Charlie's drawings and models, Augie suggested that a competent local carpenter might fit the bill. He recommended the brother of our lighting designer, Joey Patowski, the affable and muscular Newfoundland look-alike. Joey's brother Bill apparently was a very able builder who had assisted in the construction of sets at the theater on several occasions. I agreed to meet with Bill as soon as possible.

The conversation then naturally flowed from Charlie's possible replacement to a discussion of Charlie himself. Louise believed it was much more helpful to talk about one's feelings for a recently deceased friend or loved one than to keep those emotions bottled up. She told us that she had been raised by her grandparents in the Midwest, and when she had lost them, she was devastated. But talking about her strong feelings for them with others had aided her immeasurably in getting through the grieving process. Louise made us both feel so comfortable that Sophie and I did open up considerably. In the same way that I encourage actors to be truthful at an audition, so Sophie and I honestly expressed our feelings about Charlie as we sat around the convivial dinner table.

And our feelings had not always been laudatory. In somewhat similar ways, we talked about how Charlie's early reckless years had distressed and, at times, angered us. I surprised myself when I revealed how strongly disappointed and disapproving I had once been at his failure to realize his potential. But then we talked about how proud of him we had become when Charlie eventually found the strength to make a 180 degree turn.

"How terrible it must be for you then to know that he ultimately failed in his struggle," Louise gently said.

"No, I don't know that," I blurted out. "No matter how it may appear, I know that Charlie could not have so recklessly ended his life. He had worked too hard climbing out of the muck. I know that something else was behind it. I don't know what it was, but I'm going to find out, so help me."

I was amazed by my sudden outburst. Apparently it also upset Augie and Louise who stared at me with surprise for a few moments and then gave each other the strangest look. It was difficult for me to interpret that look. Tears then filled Louise's eyes, and she patted my hand.

No further word was said on this somewhat awkward subject. The conversation then turned to less controversial topics. When Sophie asked how he and Louise had met, Augie was happy to relate that they "had met cute, like in the movies." He had been in Evanston, Illinois at a medical symposium held at Northwestern seven years ago last November. When he checked into the hotel and had used the key to enter his room, he found to his chagrin that it was occupied. In fact, the very attractive and shocked occupant was about to go to bed and "looked adorable in her flannel pajamas." He of course apologized profoundly to her and received even more apologies from the flustered hotel clerk who had somehow mistakenly given him the wrong key.

"I couldn't get that beautiful gal or her pajamas out of my mind," Augie laughed. "So I sent her flowers the next day along with a written note of apology and an invitation to have dinner with me in the hotel restaurant that night. I don't know where I got the courage to do that, but I'm sure glad I did."

Louise then picked up the story. "I don't know how *I* had the courage to accept, but he had blushed so very nicely when he first saw me in the room and his note was so sweet and the yellow roses he sent happened to be my favorite, so I took the plunge and joined Augie for dinner. It also happened to be my birthday and I was at the hotel alone on business, so it was nice to have someone to share my birthday with. And, as it turned out, someone to share my life with."

After we both had expressed our delight with the story, I noted that there was a lovely arrangement of yellow roses in the sitting room. "Yes, Augie brings me a bunch every Saturday to commemorate that first date."

When we were sipping our second cup of decaf, I mentioned to Louise that she really looked familiar to me. I asked her if she had a sister I might once have met.

"No, I'm an only child I'm sorry to say. Perhaps I just have a very common looking face."

With that, we got up from the table and Sophie stated that she and I would take care of the washing up. When Louise demurred, Sophie insisted, much I must say to my irritation. So after saying goodnight, Louise went off to bed. Before he followed her, Augie took Sophie aside and they had a few words together. He then went upstairs.

When she joined me in the kitchen where I was considering how to stack the dishwasher, I asked Sophie what Augie had said to her.

"He said that I might want to advise you not to advance your theories about Charlie's death to Hazel Forrest when she gets here tomorrow. He said that she would have enough to deal with without hearing your opinions."

"Oh he did, did he? What did you say to him?"

"I told him that I appreciated his concern, but that I shared your suspicions and if we wanted to tell them to Hazel, it would be our right to do so. He seemed to accept what I said and bid me a good night."

I was a bit unsettled by what Augie had said to Sophie. Perhaps that is why I allowed Sophie to finish up in the kitchen by herself, as I thought about how foolish my words must have seemed to our hosts.

"Since you're no help at all down here," Sophie chided, "why don't you just trundle off to bed. I'll only be a few minutes more."

"Well, if you really don't mind…" I murmured as I hastily left Sophie in the kitchen.

I was in the upstairs bathroom brushing my teeth when I heard a soft knock on the door. Wondering what had happened now, I opened it to find Sophie with her finger to her lips. "Shhh! Don't say a word," she whispered. "I want to show you what I found."

Following her into my bedroom I was about to comment on how silly she was acting, when she closed the door, turned on the light and placed three torn pieces of paper on my bed. They appeared to be only a fraction of the original. The brightly colored cutout letters on them had been taken from different magazines and newspapers and had been pasted onto a white card. That card had then been torn apart. It looked for all the world like the stereotypical ransom note one had seen a hundred times in movies. Except that the three pieces of paper as Sophie had arranged them read:

CHAPTER

11

"IF YOU WOULDN'T MIND TELLING me what all this cloak and dagger rubbish is about, I would be much obliged, Sophie."

"Shhhh!" she hissed once again. "Please keep your voice down and look carefully at what I found. Please."

I lowered my voice. "And what exactly have you found? Some torn pieces of paper purloined perhaps from a waste basket? I fail to see why you're being so melodramatically mysterious."

"Not a waste basket. The trash can in the kitchen."

"Oh my apologies, Miss Marple. Now it makes perfect sense! And why, for heaven's sake, were you scavenging around our hosts' trash?"

"If you'll get off your high horse for one second, I'll tell you. I was finishing up in the kitchen and was admiring their beautiful stainless steel trash can. It's one of the new models that's fully automatic. The lid opens by itself when your hand or some trash gets within a few inches of its infrared sensor. So, I tried it out. And it worked beautifully; the lid instantly opened."

"How wonderful. Now I know what to get you for Christmas."

"Shhh!" Her imitation of a kettle full of boiling water was becoming tiresome. Sophie continued, "At first glance, the inside of the trash can looked empty. Since there must have been trash accumulated during the preparation for our dinner, apparently the bag of trash must have been removed before or during the dinner party. We were the only ones to go into the kitchen after the meal."

"I bow to your little gray cells, Monsieur Poirot."

"But," Sophie continued without acknowledging my compliment, "I then noticed that there were these three pieces of paper at the bottom of the can. The odd look of the lettering caught my eye, and I picked them up. Look at them. They must have been part of a message that had been created by pasting graphics from printed material one letter at a time on a card. The card then must have been torn into a number of pieces and thrown in the trash can. All but these three must have gone out in the trash. Outside the kitchen, there's a large dumpster. I guess that's where the trash bags are placed before they're collected."

"I hope you didn't go out there and rummage around their dumpster as well."

"No, I didn't." There was a slight pause. "Not yet anyway." She went on before I could comment further. "Why would a card that looks like it was prepared by kidnappers who didn't want their handwriting to be identified be here in the kitchen in the first place, and why was it torn to pieces in the second place?"

"Well, who knows? I'm sure there's some sensible reason for it. Perhaps it was some sort of a joke. And how do we know it was only ripped up tonight? Perhaps those three scraggly scraps have been in the bottom of the magical, mystical can for a long time and have just never been noticed."

"I don't think so." There was a gleam in Sophie's eye. "Touch the scraps."

Warily, I did. "They seem a little damp," I said.

"Ah hah! Now smell them."

"Sophie, I am not going to smell items that have been in a trash can, even one that is a marvel of infrared technology." Her look prompted me to think twice about my decision, and I distastefully sniffed the pieces of paper. "They smell faintly like onion soup," I commented.

"Exactly. And that was the soup Louise was cooking when she dropped the pot and screamed. So I don't think it's implausible that the card was in the kitchen tonight when Louise was cooking the soup. Some of the soup seems to have gotten onto the card or at least onto the three pieces of the card that remained at the bottom of the can. Did someone tear up the card tonight into many pieces and intended to throw all of the torn pieces out in the trash? If so, who and why?"

"And if the person tore up the card in the kitchen tonight, (and I'm not in any way saying, Sophie, that I agree with this wild conjecture) was this person Louise or perhaps Augie or perhaps both? And did they tear it up and throw it away because they didn't want *us* to see it and read its message?"

Sophie then said, "Perhaps we can answer these questions if we could figure out what the message might have been."

I asked, "Do you think we can decipher it only using these three pieces? I am not in any mood to go diving in that dumpster."

"Well, since you and I are both pretty good at Scrabble and crossword puzzles, let's look at them again. The way they're torn, each scrap seems to be part of a separate word. So, let's see if we can figure out what the three words might have been. Okay?" Sophie asked.

"All right, I'll play this game for a few minutes," I said reluctantly, "and then I must go to bed. What could these three words be?"

"*PY*: *Spy?* With the first letter torn off? (That would fit nicely into your "Bond, James Bond" mentality tonight, Sophie.)

THD: *Third?* With the two middle letters missing?

ISE: Part of a bad spelling of *anniversary?*

THIRD ANNIVERSARY?

No, it's not *third* because it looks like the *THD* were all one unit, pasted directly next to each other. No other letters could have been placed in between them. Or was it an abbreviation for *third?* And remember, the Freemounts have been married for *seven* years."

Sophie then continued, "*ISE* are the final letters of *surprise* and what else?"

"Well, of course, they are the final letters of *Louise*," I mentioned. "Would seeing her own name spelled out in this strange way have frightened her enough into dropping the soup? Is that too crazy?"

"It's certainly a possibility," she said. "And a pretty darned good one. Let's for the time being say that the third word is *Louise*. What could the whole message have been? Something unnerving enough to cause her to drop the pot."

Sophie then took out that ever available notebook of hers and scribbled word after possible word. I took a piece of paper and did the same. We both worked for several minutes mumbling words quietly to ourselves when suddenly I shouted:

"Shhhh!" Sophie almost smothered me with a pillow. "That certainly could be it, Harry. Congratulations!"

"Oh, no, it can't be right, Sophie. If she got this message today, it couldn't be a birthday greeting for her."

"Why not," Sophie asked.

"Because today is May 11th, and Augie and Louise told us that they celebrated her birthday on their first date in the Illinois hotel restaurant in *November*, seven years ago. And why would a birthday card, even one composed of these cutout letters have frightened Louise at all and especially one received months before her next birthday? And why would Louise and Augie want to destroy such a card anyway before we or anyone else had the chance of seeing it? No, I think we're off the mark here. None of this makes any sense. Louise and Augie have been wonderful to us. Why should we be suspicious of them?"

"Maybe you're right, Harry. But this is just another example of these bizarre coincidences and accidents that strike me as too fishy to dismiss. I'm suspicious of everyone in this screwy..."

A gentle knock at my bedroom door interrupted Sophie from finishing her thought. "Harry, is everything all right?" It was Augie whispering.

"I told you to keep your voice down," Sophie frantically mimed to me.

I quickly pushed the pieces of paper under the pillow and opened the door. "Yes, everything's fine, Augie. Sophie and I were just going over our plans for tomorrow. I'm sorry if we disturbed you."

"No problem. Louise thought something might be wrong. You know women." Augie, dressed in bathrobe and pajamas, looked quickly around the room at Sophie. "Please excuse the sexist remark, Sophie. It's late. And with my very politically incorrect foot in my mouth, I'll wish you two nice people pleasant dreams." With a smile, Augie left closing the door behind him.

I flashed Sophie an "I told you so" look and was about to reiterate how nice the Freemounts were and how unfounded were our suspicions when I saw that Sophie was concentrating on something. I followed her glance. She was staring at the bed and most specifically at the one piece of paper that was sticking out from under the pillow.

I had always considered myself a fairly articulate man with a fairly extensive vocabulary, rarely at a loss for words. So why was the only one that came out of my mouth at that moment: "Oops"?

CHAPTER
12

There is a willow grows aslant a brook,
That shows his hoar leaves in the glassy stream;
There with fantastic garlands did she come...

And there was perky Suzie McKenzie happily skipping along the embankment reciting happily her Saturday morning monologue of Ophelia's mad scene while happily holding Lucy by a leash...

There, on the pendent boughs her coronet weeds
Clambering to hang, an envious sliver broke;
When down her weedy trophies and herself
Fell in the weeping brook. Her clothes spread wide...

And now Suzie McKenzie magically morphed into Belinda dressed in the diaphanous gown she had worn when we had first met smiling beguilingly at Queen Gertrude (who looked very much like Joey Patowski) who was standing beside Lucy and Robert Gregory and Augie and Sophie and Lucille Ball and me, all of us joyously waving at her from among the bulrushes...

And, mermaid-like, awhile they bore her up:
Which time she chanted snatches of old tunes;
As one incapable of her own distress...

And now Belinda transformed herself into Louise wearing flannel pajamas since Evanston was cold in November, and Louise was sweetly singing

Happy Birthday to me

And the lyrics materialized themselves as colorful, cut out letters flying jauntily above us, and Joey and Lucy and Robert and Augie and Sophie and Lucille Ball and I all happily joined in singing

Happy Birthday to me
   but long it could not be
   Till that her garments, heavy with their drink,
   Pull'd the poor wretch from her melodious lay

Happy Birthday, dear Charlie

Happy Birthday to...
   Where's Timmy, Lassie?

Happy Birthday to...
   Where's your laptop, Charlie?

Happy Birthday to....

"Muddy death," I said aloud as I awoke in a sweat. I turned on the bedside lamp and looked at my watch. It was 2:35 in the morning. I knew I wouldn't be able to go back to sleep. I never could after I had a nightmare. And this one was worse than most. I could remember only bits and pieces of it but knew that elements of the past two days had intermingled with scenes from Shakespeare. Since my new scripts were very deliberate modern interpretations of some of the Bard's plays and themes, it made some sense that Ophelia's drowning from "Hamlet" had been linked in my mind with Charlie's.

I got up and opened the attaché case I had received on Friday, the day I flew in from New York. Enjoying once again the luxurious feel of the soft leather, I took out the scripts and skimmed through them thinking of how I would cast the plays on Tuesday.

Of the seventeen actors I had called back I would select five men and five women to be in the company with one additional man and woman as understudies. I already knew that I would cast Belinda. There was no question in my mind about that. But I had not yet fully decided on which of the other actors would be cast. I then reached for the head shots of the actors to help me remember them and their special qualities.

But I couldn't concentrate. Holding the photos in my hand reminded me of the papers I had taken from Charlie's van and had not yet examined. I removed them from my jacket pockets and sat down at the desk. I put the Google Maps itinerary aside for Sophie to mull over later and looked at the other papers. Most were receipts for recompensable expenses Charlie had racked up during his motor trip cross country to Brookfield. These were for food, motel stays, gas and the like. They seemed quite reasonable and modest.

There were a few small pieces of paper that contained what looked like hand written phone numbers and addresses on them. I would give these to Sophie as well. The area codes of these phone numbers indicated that they were from out of state.

All but one. There was one phone number that had a local area code. This number was written in ink on a different type of paper from the others. When I turned it over, I saw that it was also some sort of a receipt that had the number *00168332* printed on the top in red under the preprinted word *SILICHIPZ*. The only thing else on this side was the hand written notation: *pu 1305 DG*. I wondered what in the world was or were *Silichipz*. Visions of frolicking circus clowns doing pratfalls while munching on French fries danced in my sleep-deprived brain and I started to giggle quite moronically. Before I deteriorated any further, I quickly put this receipt aside with the intention of calling the local phone number during business hours which would not be, I looked at my watch again and groaned, for another six hours or so.

So what to do now? Those French fries I had just envisioned made me realize that a snack would not be out of order right now and perhaps a cup of herbal tea or hot chocolate might soothe me back to badly needed sleep. After all, the Freemounts had invited us to make ourselves at home.

So, donning my robe and slippers, I tiptoed out of my bedroom and down the hall to the staircase. Just as I reached the top step, I stopped. Had I heard something? I paused and listened intently. Nothing. "I really must be falling apart," I thought when I distinctly heard once again some sort of a whimpering sound. I immediately thought of poor Lucy, but, no, it wasn't an animal. Was it Louise I was hearing crying very faintly? I wasn't entirely sure, but I knew I couldn't stand there any longer. As quietly and yet as quickly as I could I descended the stairs thinking that Sophie was entirely correct. This was undoubtedly the screwiest place I had ever been unfortunate enough to visit. Debating whether or not I should now wake Sophie up to verify the source of the sound, I decided that I would satisfy my hunger first and screw these mysteries!

I was therefore more than startled when I entered the kitchen and saw Sophie sitting at the kitchen table. My rapid entrance almost made her jump out of her skin. I apologized for frightening her and then asked what she was doing there.

"I guess neither of us could sleep, boss," she said. "That damn birthday message, or whatever it is, was bothering me so much that I just had to see if there were other words on that card before it was ripped up."

"You don't mean to tell me that you went dumpster diving! Oh, Sophie how could you?"

"Before you get your knickers even more twisted, let me tell you that when I opened the dumpster's cover, I saw that it was completely empty. Either no bags of trash were in there tonight, or they had all been collected or removed before I got there about ten minutes ago."

"What do you mean removed? Removed by whom?"

"Well, I'm pretty positive that Augie noticed the letters on your bed."

"Sophie, my head is spinning from all these conspiracy theories. The next thing you'll be telling me is that it was Dr. August Freemount who was on that grassy knoll in Dallas."

"All right, you've made your point. But you can't deny that everything that has happened since we've arrived in Brookfield has given us both the jitters, and legitimately so."

I told her that indeed I could not deny that. Sophie saw me eyeing the cup of tea in front of her (chamomile) and she offered to make me one adding that it might help both of us get back to sleep. While sipping the tea and munching on another piece of the chocolate cake I had so enjoyed at dinner, I told Sophie about the contents of the paper items I had examined in my room. She also had no idea in what line of work a firm named Silichipz would be involved.

When I told her that I thought I had heard Louise crying, Sophie seemed very upset. "That poor woman. What is bothering her so? Something terrible has definitely unnerved her. She seemed perfectly fine yesterday and this morning. It must be that card she received. I have half a mind to bring up the matter directly to her and tell her we'll gladly help her with whatever it is, if she'd only confide in us."

"Remember we're guests in this house and in this town. I don't think it's advisable for us to go off half-cocked before we know exactly what we're dealing with. For all we know she could be some way responsible for the state Charlie evidently got himself into that caused him to start drinking again with such a vengeance. Though I really can't believe that. She never met Charlie, and neither did anyone else in Brookfield. Let's go about our little detective work as quietly and unobtrusively as possible and see what we unearth. What do you say, Sophie?"

I never got a chance to hear what Sophie had to say, because just at that moment the phone rang. "It's almost four in the morning. Do you think something else has happened?"

"I certainly wouldn't be surprised," Sophie said with an exasperated tone. "Listen. I can hear Augie talking on the upstairs phone. I can't make out what he's saying. Can you?"

"I'm afraid not. Perhaps it's another medical emergency." As I said this, we heard footsteps on the upstairs hall and then on the stairs.

"Oh, you two are still up," Augie said with surprise as he entered the kitchen.

"Yes, we both needed a cup of tea. Is there something wrong?" I asked.

"That was Hazel Forrest on the phone. She just landed at the airport."

CHAPTER
13

IN THE EARLY MORNING OF Monday, May 12th, my assistant and I drove to the airport to pick up Hazel Forrest, the fiancée of the deceased Charles Wetherstone. She had been advised of his death on Sunday by Dr. Freemount and had immediately flown from Portland to make arrangements for the body.

It had taken quite a bit of persuasion for Augie to agree that Sophie and I should meet Hazel Forrest at the airport and not he. He was concerned that we would worry her unnecessarily with our unfounded suspicions about Charlie's death. But we assured him that we would be on our best behavior and not add to her anxiety. We also reminded him of the full day he had in front of him and how he and Louise could both benefit from a few more hours of sleep that night. It was my mentioning Louise that I think finally made him relent, and he told us that Ms. Forrest should call him at his office in the early afternoon to coordinate the details.

"I'm still suspicious of Augie's behavior," Sophie said to me after Mandy had calmly and confidently advised us to take the second right. "I still think he's trying to hide something."

"I know you do, but until we have more concrete evidence I suggest we keep our minds, or what's left of them, as open as possible."

Sophie begrudgingly agreed to my sensible suggestion, and the conversation turned to what we would say to Hazel Forrest when we met her. "I can only imagine what sort of emotional state she'll be in," I said. "Half hysterical I would think and completely exhausted. She probably hasn't slept a wink. I've never been very good with hysterical women, I'm afraid. Maybe you should be the one to take her under your wing. What do you think, Sophie?"

"I think you've got a point there, Harry. I'll be glad to do what I can for her. And despite what the doctor says, I think enlisting her in our efforts of finding out what really happened to Charlie will be the best thing for her. I know that I always feel better when I can be proactive in a difficult situation. I bet Hazel will feel that way too."

"I hope so. We need to get as much information as we can from her about Charlie and those troubles his friend mentioned on the phone. If she knows about them, all the better. If not, she can at least identify the caller so we can contact him directly. I brought Charlie's cell phone with us so we can play the message to her if it proves necessary."

"Good. I guess we'll take her to the Inn and get her a room there. I wish it were a little nicer, but it seems to be the only place in town that's at least halfway decent. And we know for sure that they have vacancies there. Do you think," Sophie then asked, "that it would be better for *us* to check back into the Inn as well? Considering the odd things that have happened at the Freemounts?"

"Let's give that matter a lot of thought before we take the chance of insulting Augie and Louise. Remember, he's a high-muck-amuck on the theater's board of directors. We still have shows to put on there this summer, remember. The less friction we can cause the better, I would think." And, hearing the wooden clanking sounds under us, I added,

"Let's cross that bridge when we come to it." That elicited a minor groan from Sophie and put us both in a slightly better humor in the remaining time we had before we saw the signs pointing us to the airport.

When Mandy proclaimed that we had reached our destination in her self-satisfied way, we parked in the lot. There was a noticeable chill in the air as we walked through the pre-dawn darkness toward the terminal. This probably was the cause of the slight shiver I felt run up and down my spine. However, the sound of our footsteps loudly echoing through the completely deserted parking lot might have also been a contributing factor. I noticed that Sophie was looking cautiously left and right over her shoulders unconsciously mirroring my movements. We increased our pace until we finally entered the airport's arrival lounge.

I was a little dismayed to find that it too appeared to be completely empty. Without thinking, I called out, "Hello, is anyone here?" Sophie jumped a little at the sound of my voice, but other than that there was no response. We waited a minute or two. The lounge remained eerily silent.

Taking out her phone and the paper Augie had given us, Sophie called the number Hazel Forrest had provided him. On the third ring, it was answered. When Sophie heard the voice on the other end, she gave me a strange look, turned on the speakerphone, and handed the phone to me.

"Hello, hello," a low male voice repeated. A *male* voice?

"Uh, hello. I'm trying to reach Hazel Forrest." My voice clearly reflected the surprise we both felt.

"Is this Dr. Freemount?" the voice asked.

"Uh, no. It isn't. May I please speak to Hazel Forrest? Is she there?"

There was a momentary silence. Then, "She just stepped away. Who did you say this was?"

"Uh, we've come to pick Ms. Forrest up and take her to the hotel," I stumblingly said.

"I see." There was another longer pause before the man spoke again. "Come to hanger B behind the main terminal, and we'll see you there." The phone clicked off.

"Curiouser and curiouser," I muttered as I handed her phone back to Sophie.

"Listen, you might want to hang around and continue to quote Lewis Carroll, but I think we should get the hell out of here. Or call the cops. Or something," Sophie exhaled rapidly. "Who is that guy who answered the phone? And what has he done with Hazel Forrest?"

Somehow, I found the courage to say, "There's only one way of finding out." The trepidation I had felt only a moment ago had turned to the anger I had experienced seeing Charlie's body. "Nothing is going to scare me off or prevent me from finding the truth."

"Are you nuts, Harry? You're not going to march right into some deserted airline hanger in a deserted airport at five o'clock in the frigging morning and meet some strange guy who has no right being there in the first place and who has no right having her cell phone in the second place and who might have done, God knows what, to that poor girl in the third place. Are you?"

"Do you want to come with me, or should I go alone?"

Sophie looked at me in silence. Evidently the sincerity in my voice convinced her that I was serious and at least in my mind knew what I was doing.

Finally, she said, "Okay, but I'm putting 911 on my speed dial, so I'll only have one button to press, when the serial killer pounces."

I smiled my thanks, waited while she performed her cell phone mechanics, and then the two of us walked through the deserted terminal and out its rear door. The runways of this relatively small airport were in front and to the side of us as well as a number of other buildings dimly illuminated as the sun slowly began to rise in the east.

We walked in silence past a storage shed and some sort of fueling station until we saw the tin sided hangers in front of us. There were three of them, each about twenty yards apart. We then heard in the distance the faint sound of a vehicle. A truck perhaps? Yes, some sort of truck. Although the sound indicated the truck was not terribly close to us, the fact that someone was around this airport somewhere made the situation seem less like a waking dream, and I was able to take a breath. Not a deep one, but a breath nevertheless.

The early rays of the rising sun shone on the first hanger we came to. The painted sign on it identified it as Hanger C. Looking once again at Sophie, and giving her a smile as large as I could muster as well as a thumbs-up gesture, I led the way to the next hanger.

The large central door of Hanger B was closed, rolled down. This stymied us for a moment until Sophie noticed the small door to the left of the hanger. We walked to it. Taking another, deeper breath, I tried the handle. It turned, and I opened the door.

Somehow the melodramatic side of me was disappointed that the door did not ominously squeak. It opened without much of a sound, and I walked in with Sophie following close behind.

The inside of the large room was not illuminated, and I found it difficult to see anything at first. Sophie of course had the good sense to bring her bag with her, and she took out one of her penlights and clicked it on. The small beam of light moved around the walls of the hanger until it rested on a figure standing about thirty feet away, its back to us. The figure slowly turned around, and we saw it was a woman.

"Hazel?" I softly said.

Before she could reply, someone behind me roughly shoved me to the ground. "Hold it right there, Buddy," the voice said.

"NO, YOU HOLD IT, *BUDDY!* You take one more step toward me or the little lady here, and it'll be your last. You think you're a tough guy, huh, *buddy?* Well, the only real tough guy around here is this tried-and-true, trusty little 38 caliber peashooter I'm holding right here in my pocket. It's unerringly pointed right between those big baby blues of yours and is just aching to make their acquaintance. So how do you like them apples, *buddy?*"

I would have liked to have come up with something like that. But it's not easy to talk like Raymond Chandler when your face is being squashed against a concrete floor, your right nostril is squirting hemoglobin like there's no tomorrow, and the foot of what felt like an eight hundred pound gorilla is firmly pressed into the small of your back. So all that came out of my mouth was something that sounded like "Oomph."

Momentarily startled, Sophie then pulled out her cell phone to speed dial 911 when Magilla Gorilla relieved the phone from her and said, "I don't think you'll be making any calls until we find out what's going on here."

"That's exactly what I want to know," Sophie spat out.

Charleton Heston's voice manfully screaming: "Take your stinking paws off *her*, you damned dirty ape!" suddenly came into my head, but all I actually said was "Mhhh Mhhh."

"Oh, Harry, your nose is bleeding." Sophie then gave a look to King Kong who graciously allowed her to take out a tissue and hand it to me after graciously removing his Size 12 Triple E from my back."

Hearing Sophie mention my name, the woman started walking towards us. "Harry? You're Harrison Hunt?"

"I am, madam." I tried to enunciate the words with as much authority as I could muster. However, it was not easy to maintain one's dignity while sitting on one's backside on a slab of concrete with a Kleenex pressed against one's nose. "And if you are Hazel Forrest," I continued, "we have journeyed to this God-forsaken corroded Quonset hut in the middle of the night to provide you with any and all assistance we could, and this is the thanks we receive. So much for chivalry," I added under my breath.

"Frank?" the woman questioningly searched Mighty Joe Young's not so baby blues.

"No, Hazel." (Ah Ha! Her identity was finally revealed.) "We agreed. You know it's for the best."

She silently looked at the big man standing in front of her for fifteen seconds more as if deliberating, then slowly turned to me and Sophie.

"Mr. Hunt, Miss Xerxes? (Sophie nodded yes to her.) How do you do? I'm Hazel Forrest. Please let me apologize for the way we've treated you. But there is a reason for our caution and our behavior. Please let me tell you where we're coming from. Let's all sit down." She pointed to a few chairs in the corner then gave a slight smile to Sophie, to me, and finally to Frank. "Please?"

After a slight hesitation, Sophie and I did sit on the folding chairs. The look on Hazel's face somewhat softened my anger, and I became more amenable to listen to what she had to say. As she searched for the best way to begin, I could see why Charlie had fallen in love with her. She was not beautiful, not young, not instantly charismatic, but there was substance about Hazel Forrest. Yes, that was the word, substance. Her face and body revealed a life that had not been easy but had ultimately been well lived. She seemed comfortable in her own skin and satisfied with herself, her decisions, the way she had chosen to live her life. There were strength of character and strength of will evident in the way she carried herself and in her low keyed speech. As I said, substance.

"When the doctor called me yesterday and told me Charlie was dead, my whole world turned upside down. I couldn't believe it. But then when he told me the official decree was that his death was a result of an alcohol induced accident, I wouldn't believe it. And I still won't. You both had been in touch with Charlie over the years, so you know how much he had changed. Frank and I know even better than you. So after the doctor's phone call, I immediately called Frank. And he agreed with me, as I knew he would. You see, we both think... No, let me rephrase that. We both *know* that Charlie was murdered."

"Murdered?" The word startled me. "If you mean that someone's recent actions of some kind must have caused Charlie to go off the deep end again, then that is indeed what we've been thinking as well. And trying to prove."

"No, Mr. Hunt," the tall and solidly built man named Frank interrupted, "we believe that someone deliberately murdered Charlie in cold blood and made it somehow look like an accident. Nothing, no matter how terrible, would ever have made him start drinking again. I'd stake my life on that. That's why we were so cautious when you were the ones who met us here instead of the person we had expected, Dr. Freemount. For all we knew, you could have been the murderers come to get Hazel. Please accept my apology once again for all that rough stuff."

"But, I don't understand your thinking that Charlie was murdered.

The tests showed a very high blood alcohol level. Do you think the doctor was lying?" I asked.

Quietly and with complete confidence Hazel said, "We don't know yet how this murder was caused, but we know Charlie didn't cause his own death."

"We know Charlie too well. We know his fears and his demons, his struggles as well as his incredible triumphs much too well to have any doubt about this, Mr. Hunt."

It was only when Frank made this last statement that his voice finally rang a bell for me. "You're the one who left the message for Charlie last night on his cell phone. You're the one who called him *Meathead*."

They looked at me so strangely that I took out Charlie's cell phone from my jacket pocket and played the message right then and there for them on the speaker phone. I mentally kicked myself for not having recognized Frank's voice earlier. Perhaps I could have spared myself two scraped knees and a bloody nose, which thankfully had finally ceased bleeding before I had become too lightheaded.

Although daylight had not yet completely illuminated the hanger, I could clearly see that hearing Frank's ebullient and heartfelt message had caused Hazel's expressive eyes to fill. In fact, none of us was unmoved.

I then told them the whole story that related specifically to Charlie in as coherent and chronological a fashion as I could, given the early hour and the lack of sleep. Sophie helpfully inserted facts and footnotes when needed to make the commentary more complete. I related how optimistic and cheerful Charlie's emails from last week had seemed and how surprised we were that he had missed the first production meeting. I described how Lucy had led us to his body, the findings of Dr. Freemount and the police, and how we had returned last evening (was it only last evening?) to the bungalow and what we had found there and in the van and what we had not found (Charlie's laptop).

Hazel was very concerned about Lucy. I told her that someone I knew volunteered at the Animal Shelter and that he would be checking on her condition later today. As soon as I heard from Robert Gregory, I told Hazel, I would let her know.

Frank was particularly interested in the package that should be waiting for us to reclaim at the UPS office this morning. When I asked him if he knew what it contained, he said he might have an idea but would wait until he saw it before he commented further. I noticed that he had exchanged a meaningful look with Hazel when the package was first mentioned.

Before we had left Pemberley Cottage to go to the airport this morning, Sophie had placed all of the pieces of paper we had found at Charlie's van into her tote bag. Considering her suspicions of the Freemounts, she felt it prudent not to leave these possible clues behind. Frank and Hazel expressed great interest in seeing them.

"How about we first get you settled at the Inn and then you can more comfortably look at everything we've found," Sophie suggested.

On our way back to the car, Frank showed us his pretty impressive private plane. He told us he had been a longtime pilot and had instantly decided to fly Hazel here himself as soon as she had told him about Charlie.

We learned much more about Hazel and Frank (whose surname incidentally was Gerrardi) during our ride back to the Brookfield Inn. Sophie dutifully took relevant notes for us to go over later. Frank had just begun answering my questions about his cryptic remarks on the phone message to Charlie when we arrived.

It was so early that the night receptionist was still at the front desk when we entered. As she had her coat on, it appeared she was waiting to be relieved. It was the same rather mousey-looking young woman whom

I had seen a few times before. She and the manager had expressed their disappointment at our checking out Saturday.

She therefore seemed surprised when Sophie and I came up to the front desk along with a second couple. "Why, Mr. Hunt and Miss Xerxes, how nice to see you again. May I help you with something?" she shyly but politely said.

Before I could tell her that Hazel and Frank wanted to check in, the door behind the front desk was rapidly pushed open and we heard a young man's voice say, "Sorry I'm a little late this morning, sweetie baby, but you have no idea what kind of an awesome night I had last night, if you know what I mean, whoooeee!"

The young man's smirking face turned stone cold as he saw us standing there. I was as surprised as he was. I hadn't expected to see Randy Williamson until the callbacks tomorrow evening.

Chapter

15

"Whoa! Mr. Hunt, you sure did give me one heck of a start. Top of the morning to you," with a wink, Randy tipped an invisible hat to us. "You know, you're the last person I'd have guessed would be up and about so very early in the a.m. From what I've read about you, Mr. Hunt, and I've read everything I could get my hands on, you're quite the mister night owl. Not like us little itty bitty early birds scratching for that little itty bitty early morning worm. Isn't that right, Meredith?" he laughingly asked the shy girl next to him with a flash of his infectious smile.

"Um, how can I, um, help you, Mr. Hunt?" stammered the clearly embarrassed young woman looking down at her hands on the desk.

"Actually, it's our friends here who need your help," I said. "They'd like to check in if possible."

Before the young lady could respond, Randy enthusiastically bounced in. "Sure thing, Mr. Hunt. I'll be delighted to take care of you folks so that little Meredith here can go home and get her beauty sleep. Not that she needs it, of course." His smile would not have been out of place in a tooth paste commercial

"Thank you, Randy," I said trying to appear not to notice the blush that instantly engulfed the young woman's face or what I could see of it. She nodded and with a slight smile awkwardly departed through the little door behind the reception desk.

"Sweet girl, very artistic: makes collages, takes pictures, and all that type of stuff, but, boy, does she need to climb out of that shell," Randy confided to us as she closed the door behind her. "Now, let's get you nice folks registered as quickly as we can. You look plumb tuckered out, if you don't mind my saying so."

"Thank you. We are pretty tired," Hazel said.

"Just arrived from the Big Apple, like Mr. Hunt, are you?"

"No, we're from Oregon, and we'd like two rooms, please."

Randy's eyebrows shot up when he heard Hazel's request, and he handed both Frank and Hazel separate registration cards to complete. To distract him from further inquiry, I said, "I'm surprised to see you here, Randy. Have you worked at the Inn long?"

"Not too long, Mr. Hunt. It's just one of the temporary jobs I take in between gigs. Gotta pay those bills while waiting for that big break, you know."

"Or that big worm," Sophie interjected with a disapproving tone in her voice.

Not seeming to notice, Randy continued, "I guess you didn't spot me when I helped out at the dinner party the theater threw for you here at the Inn Friday night. You didn't say anything about it at the audition, so I didn't bother to mention it. I hope my having to work at these odd jobs won't put me at a disadvantage at the callbacks. I'm a serious actor, Mr. Hunt, and I've given up a lot to work on my craft. I was damned straight with you when I told you how much the chance of working with you means to me."

"I'm sure you were, Randy. And of course I realize artists have to do lots of things they'd rather not in order to make ends meet."

"That's a relief, Mr. Hunt. Say, didn't I read that when you were at Yale you had to work for a time as a bartender?"

"I certainly did. At a number of night spots I'd gladly like to forget."

"But all experience is helpful to your art, don't you agree, Mr. Hunt? The more you learn about human nature, the more you can incorporate into your performances. I've certainly learned a lot about people doing these day jobs, Mr. Hunt. And not always good; that's for damned sure. But always beneficial to my growth as an actor."

The sincerity I heard now in Randy's tone more than made up for his earlier glibness. And I remembered why I was so impressed with his audition on Saturday.

"All rightie now, Miss Forrest and Mr. Gerrardi," Randy took their completed cards, "if you would just follow me, we'll get you all settled into rooms 214 and 215. Let me help you with your bags."

We spent only a few more minutes together in Hazel's room after Randy left us. Frank thought it a good idea for all of us to get a little rest before we decided what to do next. It seemed an excellent suggestion. Before Sophie and I left, I remembered that Augie had wanted Hazel to phone him at his office later to work out arrangements. The look in her eyes as I said that last word made me take her hand and hold it for a few seconds.

"We're here for you, Hazel, and we'll do anything we can to help," I said.

"Just help us find out who hurt my Charlie. That's all I want," she whispered.

"You have my word," I said.

Sophie gave Frank the stack of papers she had been holding in her bag to review, and saying so long to Randy at the desk, we got back in the car and headed on our way back to the Freemounts' to catch a few more winks ourselves.

We were discussing our quite different reactions to Randy Williamson (Sophie was less of a fan than I was) when Sophie suddenly called out, ""Stop the car, Harry." I did so, and Sophie pointed to the storefront across the street. The sign printed in stylish red letters on the window read: *Silichipz- For All Your Computer Needs.*

"Computers?" I asked mystified.

"Of course! What dummies we are. It must be their clever way of shortening silicon chips."

The light bulb finally lit above my befuddled brain when I heard Sophie's explanation, and I smiled as I crossed the street with her. I was sure that we had just found the whereabouts of Charlie's missing laptop. Looking in the window, it was obvious that the store was closed.

"It won't open for at least a couple of hours," Sophie said. "We left the receipt with Frank anyway. We'll get it later." She took out her notebook and wrote down the computer store's address: 25 Commerce Street.

Seeing her notebook reminded me that with all that had happened Sophie and I had not had the opportunity yet of discussing the sudden appearance of Hazel and Frank. "There's a little coffee shop over there that looks like it's open. What do you say we sit down and try to put things in their proper perspective? I'd like to go over those notes you took on the way to the Inn about what Hazel and Frank said to us."

"Sounds like a plan, boss, and a good one. And, man, could I use another cup of tea."

Meals was the name of the cozy little coffee shop. It looked like it had just opened for breakfast, and the sole waitress seemed not too wide awake as she seated us at one of the half dozen still empty booths. We ordered two cups of tea, and I also chose one of the tempting French crullers on display. Sophie ordered whole wheat toast. As we looked over Sophie's notes, I remembered how Hazel had told us she had met Charlie.

"I was a drunk, "she had calmly and bluntly stated. "My life was pretty much in a shambles when I finally got sense enough to go to A.A. The meetings and my sponsor were what I needed, and the day that I celebrated my 365th day without a drink, I received the greatest gift of my life: I met Charlie."

She told us how they had talked after his first meeting. She told us how much they both had in common. She told us how and why she had introduced him to Frank who had become Charlie's sponsor.

"I was tough with him," Frank continued the story, "as tough as my sponsor had been to me. I wouldn't let him off the hook, wouldn't let him fool himself about how much work he needed to do, about how rough the process would get, about how much pain he had to go through before it would start to get better. But Charlie never complained. He never slowed down. I've never met anyone more motivated to change his life. And the strongest reason Charlie had for working so hard was Hazel. With her beside him, he couldn't give up."

"And with him beside me, I couldn't give up on myself," Hazel said simply. "Neither of us had ever known such friendship, such camaraderie. And the day that Charlie knew for sure that he was capable of giving love to others and acknowledged that he deserved receiving it back was the day that I went with him to the pound. Caring for Lucy, taking responsibility for her welfare and being able to accept her unconditional love carried Charlie to greater and greater growth. And somehow during these years, our friendship changed to love, to a mature and deep relationship that neither of us had ever before experienced or had even known was possible."

We had reached Sophie's last entry in her notes: *Then troubles began?*

She clarified the notation. "That's when you started to ask Frank to explain that remark he made on the phone message. And that's when we arrived at the Inn. They said they'd explain further after they got some rest."

"Right. And speaking of rest, we better get some too. I feel like a ..." Before I could complete the clever and apposite simile I noticed that a man who had recently entered the coffee shop was standing over me staring very strangely. I was about to ask him if I could be of some assistance when I saw that he was holding in his hand a local newspaper. He had been looking at the front page and then turning back to me. I looked down to try to see what was so fascinating in the paper when I clearly saw my face grinning back at me.

16

NEW YORK DIRECTOR BRINGS DEATH TO BROOKFIELD

An editorial by Damian Devoe

We've all heard about the debauched life style that goes on behind the bright lights of Broadway. We've all heard about the drunken orgies, the rampant drug use, the licentious, unbridled hanky panky that takes place on the infamous casting couch.

Many of us might have assumed that these scandalous reports of out-of-control behavior along Manhattan's so-called Great White Way were just unsubstantiated rumors.

Many of us charitably might have viewed these tales as mere tabloid hyperboles, egregious exaggerations created to sell scandal sheets and garner huge television ratings.

Many of us might have been willing to give these Big Apple so-called artistes the benefit of the doubt.

And then the Brookfield Players in their good intentioned naiveté decided to hire portly New York City director Harrison Hunt to oversee the summer season at their Barn Theater.

And the wild rumors turned out to be not so wild after all.

Only two days after this notorious New York City director arrived in our fair city, the Brookfield police department reported the bloodied corpse of one of Harrison Hunt's own entourage drowned due to "an alcohol induced" fall.

The lifeless body of Charles Henry Wetherstone was found face down in Brookfield Creek late Sunday afternoon.

Surprisingly, the body was discovered by no one other than Harrison Hunt himself and his curvaceous female "assistant".

Astonishingly, the victim, a set designer with a reportedly long history of substance abuse, was Harrison Hunt's own personal choice for the responsible position of technical director at the Barn Theater this summer.

Both of these so-called New York City "professionals", Harrison Hunt and the now tragically deceased Charles Henry Wetherstone, were hired by the board of directors of the Brookfield Players even though many other local and qualified Brookfield residents had applied for the positions at the theater.

We wonder if any of the Barn Theater's board members are regretting their decision to bring these "Fun City" interlopers into our peaceful, law abiding community?

We wonder what other tragic occurrences will happen next?

Putting down the two copies of this morning's *Brookfield Bugle* we had just purchased from the now silently staring waitress, my "curvaceous female 'assistant'" and I were also speechless. Speechless with astonishment.

After a long pause in which we tried to process what we had just read, Sophie asked with a grin, "Another cruller?"

"Sure, why the hell not? I can see tomorrow's headline now: 'Portly Manhattan Director Undermines Town's Nutritious Eating Habits.' Oh, Sophie, when will I cease to be surprised and dismayed by the cruelty and ignorance of people?"

"And especially by the objective and fair-minded press. All the news that's fit to *mis*print!" she scoffed.

"I wonder who this Damian Devoe is anyway and why he has this xenophobic beef against me." When the waitress guardedly approached us with our bill, I asked her what she knew about him. Dawn (I saw her name embroidered on her uniform above her ample left breast) cautiously revealed that Mr. Devoe had been the editor and publisher of the local rag since he had retired from the area's community college where for many years he had taught theater arts and playwriting. Thanking Dawn for the information and swearing to her that I was neither a moral degenerate nor a debauched souse, Sophie and I left the coffee shop.

There were more people on the street now and by the stares that we received, it appeared that the *Bugle* was everyone's favorite source for hard hitting journalistic exposés.

As we got into the car as quickly as we could, Sophie ironically said, "Wasn't it Shakespeare who said 'All publicity is good publicity.'"

"Actually," I said, "it was another great poet and playwright, Brendan Behan. And I believe the exact quote was: 'All publicity is good, except an obituary notice.' And why do I feel that I've just read mine? Anyway, I'll bet you dollars to donuts (and please no references to that *portly* crack) that the good professor was one of the 'qualified' local residents who applied for the job I got."

"I think you would easily win that bet. Well, shall we go back to the Freemounts' before we're tarred and feathered and put on the next stagecoach heading east?"

"Very good idea. Home, Mandy."

We talked about a number of things on our drive back. We wondered how the actors we would be seeing tomorrow night would feel about the fair and unbiased newspaper editorial. I had been treated as a hero by them after the Robert Gregory collapse. I wondered if their opinion of me had now been irreversibly changed.

Another thought came to me, and I said, "You know, Sophie, I wouldn't be at all surprised if *herr professor* will turn out to be the *Bugle's* respected and influential drama critic as well as editor. I certainly look forward to his impartial and objective opening night reviews of our productions. To quote another treasured Behan gem: 'Critics are like eunuchs in a harem; they know how it's done, they've seen it done every day, but they're unable to do it themselves.'"

"And you swore to that waitress you weren't a moral degenerate," Sophie said as we finally made it back unscathed to Pemberley Cottage.

Both cars were in the driveway when we arrived, and the house was quiet. We tiptoed up to our rooms so as not to disturb either Louise or Augie. Both Sophie and I slept the sleep of the innocent (so there, Damian Devoe) for several hours. The Brandenburg Concerto woke me. Looking at my watch, I was astonished that it was almost noon.

Hazel was calling to let me know she and Frank had gotten some needed sleep as well and were now in a much better state to proceed. As we all were eager to see that package that had been sent to Charlie, she suggested that we meet at the UPS store. She read the address off the notice to me and said that Randy had assured her that it was within walking distance of the Inn. I told her we should be there in about half an hour. As she hadn't mentioned the newspaper editorial, I didn't mention it to her. The door to the Freemounts' bedroom was open, and I saw that the bed had been made. I then looked out the window and saw that both of their cars were no longer in the driveway.

I knocked at Sophie's door and told her Hazel's plan. She and I met in the kitchen ten minutes later, downed some juice and the quick sandwich Sophie put together and were about to head out the door when my cell phone rang again.

It was difficult at first to determine who it was who was calling me. There was very loud background noise that interfered with my understanding what was being said. It took me a minute or two before I finally deciphered that it was Belinda. She sounded terribly distraught. Images of how she had looked the night of her breakdown three years ago flashed before me. My attempts to calm her down seemed not to be working, and all I could really make out over the phone were the words. "Harry, you've got to help." I told her I would do anything to help and repeatedly asked where she was. I put her on speaker phone so that both Sophie and I could listen and try to interpret what she was saying.

Finally a man's voice came on the phone. "Hello," he said, "I don't know who you are, but the lady here is in very bad shape. I saw her crying so hard on the phone that I came over and asked her if I could help. She just handed the phone over to me."

"Who are you and where are you?" I said in a panic.

"My name is Joe Flaherty. I'm the bartender here at *The Green Parrot.*"

"The Green Parrot?"

"Yeah, it's a little bar and grill over here on Mercer Street. I think you'd better come down here and try to help your friend."

I got the complete address and told the bartender that I would be there as fast as I could. Thanking him profoundly for his assistance, I hung up the phone.

"I think I know where Mercer Street is," I told Sophie. "I'm sure we passed it coming back from the hospital, but I'll set the GPS to lead us there directly. Oh, I guess I should call Hazel to tell her we'll be delayed."

"Listen, Harry, why don't you drive me to the theater so I can pick up my car. Then I'll go on and meet them at the UPS store, and you can head on to find Belinda. If you need my help, just give me a call," Sophie said.

That seemed like a sensible plan, and we headed off to the theater. In the car, I asked Sophie if she had been able to understand any of the words Belinda had said after I had turned on the speaker.

"It was very hard to hear clearly. The music was playing so loudly in the background. But I think I made out what sounded like the words *Robert* and *Blood*."

CHAPTER 17

IN THE THEATER'S PARKING LOT, Sophie turned to me, touched my arm and said, "Don't worry, Harry. Whatever's happened, she'll come through it with flying colors. She's done it before." Have I mentioned how fortunate I am to have Sophie in my life?

Through my rear view mirror, I saw Sophie get into her beetle as I sped off (considerably faster than the posted speed limit) for 44 Mercer Street and whatever waited for me there. Out of the corner of my eye I saw someone wave to me a few minutes later (it might have been the lighting designer Joey Patowski) but I didn't stop or even slow down and took the second left as Mandy instructed. I thought I heard a few horns blaring at me and probably broke more than one traffic law as I whisked through downtown Brookfield. I was (How had Randy put it at the audition? Oh, yes.) *sweating bullets* as I eventually followed Mandy's final direction and saw the rather seedy looking building in front of me. Of course there was no parking space anywhere near *The Green Parrot*, so I double parked, more than likely illegally (Isn't that what we *"Fun City* interlopers" do?) and entered the bar at full gallop.

I was instantly double whammied by both the frigid blast of the air conditioning and the eardrum-bursting blaring dissonance of the rock music. Momentarily disoriented, I tried in vain to spot Belinda while my eyes slowly adjusted to the darkened interior. Although not mobbed, there were enough customers milling around to prove distracting. I finally made it to the long mahogany bar and tried to get the bartender's attention. I called out several times before he noticed me.

"Yes sir, what can I do for you?" he said with a smile as he approached me.

"Are you Joe Flaherty?" I frantically asked.

Noticing how upset I was, he nodded and said, "You're the guy I spoke to on the lady's phone?"

"Yes, I am. Please show me where she is."

The smile on his weathered face had clouded over as he mumbled something I couldn't quite catch. I repeated my request and this time I heard him distinctly say, "I'm sorry, buddy, I can't."

"You can't? What do you mean, you can't? Where is she?"

"I'm afraid she's gone."

Gone? Gone? No, she couldn't be gone. That's crazy. I must have heard it incorrectly. After all it's so noisy in here. Perhaps what he actually said was: she'll be back anon, or she seemed very withdrawn, or she's in the john, or on the lawn, or in the salon, or…

"Did you say she's *gone*?"

"I'm afraid so, buddy. Right after I hung up with you, I turned around and she had, like, vanished, you know, disappeared. I looked in all the rooms, went outside and looked all around, even had one of the girls check the ladies' room. Nope. She was gone."

"But did she say anything, tell anyone where she was going?"

"I'm afraid not, buddy. One minute she was standing right behind me; the next minute she was gone. All she left was this." He handed me Belinda's cell phone which he retrieved from behind the bar. "Sorry, buddy."

"Thank you. I'm sorry to have caused you all this trouble." I think I said something like this to the bartender, but truthfully I have no memory of what I said, or if I said anything at all. I slowly walked out of *The Green Parrot* and got into my car double parked in front. And sat there. My mind was racing. Where would she have gone? Why would she have gone? Was she all right? What was going on?

And then I found myself reliving the last time Belinda had disappeared. Three years ago we were rehearsing a highly anticipated production of The Scottish Play and Belinda was dazzling in rehearsals as Lady Macbeth. Both she and I were enjoying working together again.

After a string of hit plays off and on Broadway in which I had cast Belinda as leading lady, she had accepted an offer to go to Hollywood and begin a film career. I of course remained in New York. The separation proved difficult for our relationship, and we had begun dating others. Still, I felt more than a twinge of regret when I had heard that Belinda had married on the coast. I was delighted when she contacted me about six months later to tell me that for business reasons she and her industrialist husband would be moving back east. I had just been offered to direct this show at Lincoln Center, and it seemed fortuitous indeed that she was now available to do it. I was as charmed as everyone else was by Luke, her husband, when I met him when he came to take Belinda home occasionally after rehearsal. He seemed the most loving, the most affable of husbands. They seemed the most devoted and radiant of couples.

Then one day, out of the blue, Belinda had disappeared. She had not shown up for rehearsal. She hadn't called either Sophie or me. There was no answer when we tried to reach her. This was not at all like Belinda, and as the day turned to evening, we all had become quite concerned.

I was in my apartment having my third glass of wine when the phone rang. It was Sophie. "Turn on channel four," she somberly said.

The television reporter was standing outside Belinda's townhouse on Sutton Place. He had announced that an unidentified woman had been found walking in a daze through the streets of the West Village that afternoon. She had been dressed only in a nightgown and was barefoot. The front of her nightgown had been covered in blood. She had been taken to Bellevue Hospital. An hour ago a night nurse at Bellevue had come on duty and had identified the woman in the psychiatric ward as her favorite stage actress, Belinda Bobbie. "I've seen all of her performances," the nurse had gushed. Members of the New York City Police Department's Sixth Precinct had then visited Ms. Bobbie's townhouse on Sutton Place. When they received no answer, they obtained a search warrant and broke down the front door. The naked body of Luke Halpert, the well-known businessman and husband to Ms Bobbie, was found in the master suite in a pool of blood. He had been fatally stabbed with a kitchen knife.

When Sophie and I got to Bellevue, there were scores of reporters standing outside. When they started to crowd around us, a kindly officer escorted us inside and up to the psychiatric wing. I was about to introduce myself at the desk, when there was a flurry of activity in the corridor behind me. There were shouts and curses and then suddenly Belinda burst into the lobby moaning and jabbering gibberish. She was grabbed from behind by attendants who tightened the dangling sleeves of the straitjacket around her. She was twisting and writhing in a fruitless attempt to avoid their grasp when she happened to look up and see me. The grief and suffering in her royal blue eyes formed the core of countless nightmares for me ever since.

A tap on the car door brought me out of my reverie. It was Joey Patowski.

"Hey there, Mr. Hunt. How ya doin'? I thought I saw you driving through town a little while ago. I'm going to indulge in a short one before I go back to the slave mine. Care to join me?"

"Thanks very much, Joey, but I think I'll pass. May I have a rain check?"

"Sure thing, Mr. Hunt. Anytime. I want to thank you for considering my baby brother Bill for the TD job. Dr. Freemount called him this morning and asked if he'd be interested. Bill told him it would be his pleasure to help us all out, if you thought he'd be able to do the job."

"I look forward to meeting Bill maybe in a day or two."

"Of course, you just take your time, pumpkin. I know what a shock you must be feeling. I read about Mr. Wetherstone's death in the paper. So terrible. You pay no mind to all that rubbish that lily-livered fancy pants Damian Devoe spouts out his blow hole. Since he lost out on directing his own crappola plays this summer, he's been spewing nothing but venom. Please don't for a minute think that everyone in this town is a snake like Devoe. You've got friends here, Mr. Hunt. And you can count on that."

"Thank you, Joey. You don't know how much I appreciate that. But if you'll excuse me I've got to go now and locate a lost actress, if you'll believe it."

"You don't mean Belinda Bobbie, do you?" Joey asked.

When I gulped an affirmative, she said, "Why, I just saw her drive into the Animal Shelter a couple of miles from here. She sure looked like she had a lot on her mind."

CHAPTER 18

ANIMAL SHELTER? OF COURSE! BELINDA'S brother Robert had promised to check on Lucy after he was released from the hospital today. Had he gone there already? Had something happened between Belinda and Robert that caused her to become so upset? Had something happened to Lucy? Why had Belinda gone into *The Green Parrot* and then left immediately after handing her cell phone to the bartender? Was she now on her way to meet Robert at the Animal Shelter?

I got the exact directions from Joey, thanked her again, and then drove off. I called the hospital while driving and found out that Robert Gregory had indeed been discharged late this morning. Unfortunately, the woman to whom I spoke had no more information to tell me. She didn't know whether or not Belinda or anyone else had picked him up.

As I ended this phone conversation, I saw a sign directing me to the Shelter. I followed a winding dirt road for about a quarter of a mile until I saw the first of several metal outbuildings. Belinda's sports car was standing empty in front of the shed. I parked next to it, got out and called her name twice but heard nothing but dogs barking in the distance. I was not surprised to notice that there was a hint of panic in my voice. About twenty feet to the right there was a large wooden sign stuck in the ground. I walked over to it and read: *Brookfield County Animal Shelter and Thrift Shop*. I called Belinda's name once more but again received no reply. The slight echo that reverberated back did nothing to dissipate the unease I was feeling. I hurriedly walked up the narrow path that bisected a grassy field until I came to the thrift shop. A small sign indicated that its hours of operation were from 1 to 3 pm. I checked my watch and was relieved to see that it was now ten minutes past one. As I turned the handle, I felt a bit of the peeling paint come off in my hand. I grunted with frustration when to my dismay I found that the door was locked. I spied a doorbell and rang it impatiently several times. There was no answer. I waited a minute or so and then rang it twice again.

"Hold your horses, honey, I'm coming," a voice called to me. I turned and saw a woman of indeterminate age with flaming red hair walking toward the thrift shop holding a large mewing cat in her arms. "You sweet little thing, Rhoda, we've all gotten a bit behind schedule, haven't we now, honey, but we'll fix everything, you can bet on that. Now be a good girl and stop twisting and turning while I fiddle with this darned key. It always sticks a little, doesn't it, honey?" she continued to address the cat as she finally unlocked the door and opened it. As she replaced the piece of leather on which the key was hanging back around her neck, I said to her, "Excuse me, but I'm looking for…"

"Yes, Rhoda, I know what's getting you so riled up. It's time for that little old bad pricking thing, isn't it now, honey. And I know you don't like that little old bad pricking thing one little bit, but you know it's got to be, don't you, honey." While saying this, she had walked inside, turned on the lights, and sat down at the front table.

I had no choice but to follow her in. "Pardon me, but could you tell me…" I tried to finish my sentence but once again was interrupted by the woman's ongoing monologue to the cat in her arms.

"Now then, Rhoda, honey," she said as she removed a hypodermic needle from a bag on the table and filled it from a small bottle, "you be a good girl and just pretend you don't feel a thing when this bad little old pricking thing sticks you right here behind your sweet little neck. Here it comes, honey, now it won't hurt more than a little bitty second, but it'll do you all the good in the world." Her droning on seemed to work as the cat only uttered a tiny mew as the needle was briefly injected. "There now, honey, what a brave little Rhoda you were. What a good girl, now go out and find Lion and Grapefruit and maybe you'll find a treat waiting for all of you when you come back. There you go, you sweet little thing."

"Now, what can I do for you, honey?" she turned to me with a grin. "Thank you for being so patient while I gave Rhoda her little bitty insulin shot. Twice a day, she has to get it, twice a day, and I'm sorry to say I've gotten way behind schedule today. There's been so much hubbub today, don't you know."

"Hubbub?"

"That's just the word for it, honey, just the word. First all that photographer and those newspaper reporters came round flashing their flashbulbs and asking so many questions about that sweet little thing."

"Newspaper reporters?"

"Yes, two fellas and one little gal just flashing her camera and asking so many darned fool questions that I couldn't for the life of me begin to answer. Isn't it nice that in this day and age gals get to do all the things that only fellas used to be allowed to do. Take my sister, for instance. My sister, Sally. She's a builder, can you believe that? Back in Florida she's a builder. Builds these housing developments, don't you know. And a few years back only fellas would be allowed to build those things. But now it's a new world, don't you think, honey? She wanted me to go in with her in her building business. She said to me, 'Rory, honey, now why don't you come in with me, we'll both make a killing.' That's just what she said, but I told her, 'Sally, honey, I like it much better up here where the weather is not always so hot, not always the same.' I like having four seasons, don't you know. So even though she begged me..."

"Excuse me for interrupting, but you said reporters came here today? Why?"

"Why? To see that little doggie, that's why. The one who was so brave and tried to save her master when he killed himself..."

"You mean, Lucy?" I said with my heart in my mouth.

"Why of course. Who else? Say, is that why you've come as well? Hasn't there been enough hubbub over that poor little thing? First those danged reporters and then all the others and now you. I think that it will be the best for that poor little thing if all you nosey people just left her alone and let her be. First she had to have the bad luck of having a drunk for a master and then..."

"Excuse me. You said that other people came today about Lucy after the reporters came?"

"That's right, honey. First there was that fella who volunteers here quite often. I had heard he was in the hospital but he made it his business to come out here and ask to see her. I told him that poor little thing should be left alone, but he insisted."

"You mean Robert Gregory?"

"That's right, honey. That's his name all right. He seemed a nice enough fella, but he wouldn't listen when I told him that poor little thing had had enough excitement this morning. But he insisted, so I let him go off by himself. I had to see to changing that dressing on that poor little chestnut foal that just came in last week, why she's the..."

"When did Mr. Gregory come?"

"Oh, about an hour ago, I would imagine. About fifteen minutes before that blond gal came up to me at the barn and asked me if that fella was here. When I told her he had gone back by himself to the exercise yard where we had put Lucy when the reporters had come, she went back there as well. I told her that there had been too much excitement already today for that poor little doggie, but she didn't pay me any mind. She just turned around and headed back there without as much as a by-your-leave. These gals today. They get to do anything they want, but they've lost something as well. They've lost just a little of the feminine virtues, don't you know. My sister's daughter Emmy, as an example..."

"So the blonde woman is still back there with Mr. Gregory and the dog?"

"No, and that's just the funniest thing. Just a few minutes later, as I was leaving the barn, I'm sure I saw her run back to her car. I heard the car start and drive away. But I was too busy to think much about that, because I was going to the main building to find Rhoda. She gets a little bitty insulin shot twice a day, don't you know. And we had gotten a bit behind schedule today due to all these interruptions. Now I hope you don't want to see that poor little doggie as well. I think she has had way too much excitement... Hey, there honey, where are you going?"

But I had already left the thrift shop and had started running off in the direction of the exercise area the woman had pointed to during her endless monologue. It was about twenty square feet of earth surrounded by a chain link fence, and as I got nearer to it, I could see a small body huddled in one corner near the locked gate. It was Lucy, and she was alone. And she was whimpering. And she was frantically chewing at her front right paw. And there was blood on the ground in front of her.

But where was Belinda and where was Robert? I looked frantically around but could see no one else. I called Belinda's name but once again got no answer. Where were they? What had happened? I forced myself to calm down and take a breath.

Suddenly I had an idea. I took out Belinda's cell phone from my jacket pocket, turned it on, searched the phone's directory (the way

Sophie had done on Charlie's phone) and located Robert's name. When I clicked on it, I held my breath. For four or five seconds time stood still. Then I heard it. His cell phone could be heard ringing faintly to the right. I followed the sound till I reached another outbuilding. I walked behind it and saw Belinda on the ground cradling her brother's body in her arms. They were in the same position that Augie and Louise had been in their kitchen. Only this time there was a difference. It was clear that Robert was dead.

Chapter

19

After we met Ms. Forrest at the airport, we drove her to the Brookfield Inn where she checked into a room. Ms. Xerxes and I then returned to the Freemounts' home for a few hours sleep. Around noon, I received a phone call from Belinda Bobbie. I drove to the Brookfield Animal Shelter where I located her on the grounds. She had just discovered her brother's dead body. The police and Dr. Freemount were called.

When Belinda noticed me standing in front of her, she raised her head. The indescribable grief that filled her royal blue eyes eclipsed everything else around me until the slight twisting of her body revealed the kitchen knife extruding from Robert Gregory's t-shirt covered chest. My mind instantly flashed back to the medical examiner's photograph of the body of Belinda's husband. How could it be a coincidence that both men were stabbed to death in the same way with similar looking knives?

I stood there looking down at Belinda holding Robert in her arms for what seemed an eternity. My brain was racing. What should I do? Should I go back to the thrift shop and ask for assistance? Should I call the authorities myself? (Suddenly Raymond Chandler once again took over my thought waves.) Or should Belinda and I fly the coop? Take it on the lam? Make a break for it? Do a bunk? Take a powder? Give the coppers the shake? Give the fuzz the slip? (My brain was in free fall.) Ride the midnight express? Get her *On a slow boat to China/ All to myself alone/ Out on the briny/ With the moon big and shiny…*

I don't know what would have happened if at that second my cell phone hadn't rung. It was Sophie. The phrase *saved by the bell* had never been so applicable.

"Harry, we picked up the package at UPS as well as the laptop from the computer store. Apparently the keyboard had frozen, so Charlie had left it there to be repaired when he first arrived in town. He … What did you say? I can't make it out. Your voice sounds so strange … Harry? … Did you find Belinda at the bar? How is she? … Harry? … Harry? … What? … Oh, my God! … Where? … The Brookfield what? … Oh, Animal Shelter…and what? … Oh, Thrift Shop. I see… Harry, you just stay there and try to stay calm. I'll call the police, and we'll be there as soon as we can. All right, Harry? … Oh, dear God, I'm so sorry … Harry, please take care of yourself until I get there. Please?"

The police cars and ambulance took only what seemed like moments to get to us. And seemingly right behind them were Sophie and Hazel and Frank. Seemingly only seconds then elapsed before Augie Freemount appeared. While time had slowed down and almost stopped after I found Belinda and Robert, it now happily sped up faster and faster. I think it was something that Augie gave me that made everything proceed at a surprisingly pleasurable clip until I happily closed my eyes and slept.

And there was Dr. Freemount saying to his wife Louise, "I have two nights watch'd with you, but can perceive no truth in your report. When was it she last walk'd?"

Louise answered, "Since her husband left Sutton Place, I have seen her rise from her bed, throw her nightgown upon her, unlock her bedroom door, take forth paper, fold it, write upon't, read it, afterwards tear it into shreds, and again return to bed, yet all this while in a most fast sleep." Louise pulled from out of a steaming pot three pieces of paper containing brightly cutout letters, handed them to her husband and then suddenly screamed, "Lo you, here she comes!" dropping the pot which splattered onion soup over the approaching barefoot figure clad in a becomingly slinky nightgown. The figure whose face was covered with a filmy lace veil emerged from the shadows holding Lucy on a tartan plaid leash. When the splotches of soup on her lingerie suddenly turned blood red, she released the leash and rubbed her hands in the liquid.

Cradling his wife in his arms, Augie noted, "Look how she rubs her hands!"

The glamorous veiled figure said, "Yet here's a spot."

Sophie wearing a penlight in her hair shone the light on her little notebook and said, "*Hark*, she speaks, I will set down what comes from her, to satisfy my remembrance the more strongly." When Lucy then uttered her own two cents worth, Sophie admonished her, "I said *hark*, not *bark*." Abashed, Lucy softly began to whimper and chew on her front paw.

The figure then began chanting, "Out damned spot: out I say. One: Two: Why then 'tis time to do't."

As soon as she said "One", the dead body of Belinda's husband Luke began walking like a zombie from out of the menacing shadows. When she said "Two", Robert Gregory wearing his loose fitting hooded sweatshirt entered from the opposite direction like Frankenstein's monster. Both ghouls then simultaneously slowly pulled out the kitchen knives from their chests and threw the bloody weapons into the creek below them.

As the knives fell, Charlie's body rose from the boiling onion soup-filled creek and began humming the theme from *I Love Lucy*. Hazel dressed like Lucy Ricardo skipped happily over to greet Charlie accompanied by Joey Patowski dressed as a dowdy Ethel Mertz and a now bald Frank Gerrardi outfitted as Ethel's husband Fred. There was a green parrot perched on Fred Mertz's shoulder.

The veiled figure pointed to the bleeding Luke and said, "The Thane of Fife had a wife: where is she now?" Rubbing her hands once again she asked, "What, will these hands ne'er be clean? Here's the smell of the blood still." And then she turned to the walking corpse of Robert Gregory and pulling out a royal blue spray bottle pumped the bulb releasing the sweet scent I shall always associate with Belinda and moaned, "All the perfumes of Arabia will not sweeten this little hand."

As Augie whispered to Louise "Heaven knows what she has known", the figure slowly began to raise the lacey veil from off her face. But before she could reveal her identity, a hand grasped my arm. I turned and saw Belinda behind me. She plaintively said, "Harry, you've got to help." If it was Belinda who was standing behind me, who was the veiled figure in the nightgown in front of me? I turned back and saw the figure finally uncover her face. It was someone I vaguely remembered from years ago, someone who in some vague way resembled Louise Freemount, someone who took the three torn pieces of paper from Augie's hands and placed them in mine.

It was too dark to read the words, so I ran over to Sophie and asked her to shine her penlight on them. She did, and I read the words formed from the cutout letters:

And then I woke up and saw Sophie sitting next to my bed. "Welcome back to the world of the living, boss. How are you feeling?" There was a worried look on her face.

"A little groggy I think but where…"

"You're in the hospital. You were practically in a state of shock when we got to you, and Augie gave you something to make you sleep. You were brought here a couple of hours ago."

"And Belinda, how is she? Where is she?"

"She was in a very bad way, as you know."

"Of course she was. You can imagine what finding her brother's body must have done to her. Look what it did to me," I said.

"Right, Harry. She also was taken here to the hospital. Augie seems to be very worried about her condition."

I started to get up. "Well, I'd like to see her now. Maybe I can help in some way."

Sophie held my arm. "Whoa, I think it would be much wiser for you to rest up some more. And besides… " She hesitated.

"Besides what, Sophie?" I demanded with some irritation.

"You won't be able to see her now anyway. There's a police guard stationed outside her room."

CHAPTER
20

WAS IT ALL HAPPENING AGAIN? This inescapable thought flashed through my mind as soon as Sophie told me that the police were holding Belinda under suspicion in her hospital room. Would all the investigations, the inquiries, the tabloid frenzy that took place in New York three years ago happen once again in Brookfield? Would Belinda once again be considered a major suspect in the death of a man she deeply loved?

I had thought that the unresolved questions I had about Belinda's involvement in her husband's death had finally been put to rest two evenings ago when I met her at the theater. During our long talk on Saturday Belinda had, I thought, truthfully confided all she knew about Luke's death. She told me that for a number of weeks after she had been discovered wildly wandering around Greenwich Village dressed only in a bloodstained nightgown she had been unable to remember anything at all about the incident.

Slowly, over time, bits and pieces of her memory began to return. She remembered going back to her townhouse on Sutton Place after an exhausting day of rehearsal. She and Luke had eaten an early dinner, and then he had left for an evening business meeting. Belinda had taken a mild sleeping pill to ensure herself a good night's rest and had slept soundly until she had been awakened before dawn by some noise in the house. Still feeling a bit drugged from the sleeping pill, she dazedly staggered into the living room and could barely see that there was someone in the darkened foyer about ten yards away. Belinda then believed she called out, and the person suddenly turned towards her. She then heard what she swore sounded like a church bell chime and then, as if in a dream, watched the figure slowly walk towards her. When he entered a shaft of moonlight shining through a living room window she saw his face. It was Luke. He softly whispered to her, "Forgive me, Belinda" and moved a step closer. In stunned silence she watched the moonlight reveal in agonizing slow motion more of his naked body. When the light finally fell on the knife in his chest, she screamed. The sound of her scream resounding through the silent room was the last thing she remembered until she felt the attendants at Bellevue beginning to strap the straitjacket on her. She then hysterically ran from them until she suddenly saw me. The last thing she remembered before she collapsed once again was seeing the pain in my eyes.

Mercifully, her fragile mental state prevented her from being cognizant of the media furor that then followed. The *Post*'s **BELINDA BOBBIE IN BOOBIE HATCH** and *The Daily News*' **BALMY BELINDA: BUTCHER OF BROADWAY?** were only two of the countless lurid headlines splattered across newsstands for the next few weeks.

Police and medical investigations were extensive, exhaustive and ultimately, surprisingly inconclusive. Neither the district attorney's office nor the coroner's report was able to establish whether Luke Halpert's death was self inflicted or caused by another party. The chief medical examiner said at a news conference that two to five percent of all suspicious deaths nationwide were never able to be classified as either a homicide or a suicide. And so, the grand jury had no choice but metaphorically shake its head, shrug its shoulders and go home with its bedraggled tail between its legs.

From time to time over the next few years the media tried to reopen the case. When news was leaked that Luke had not been at a business meeting that tragic night after all but had instead been ensconced with an unidentified hooker in a sleazy hotel in Queens, the motive for murder was triumphantly posited by the media for a few days. But this was once again quashed by the powers that be, and the rapacious phoenix reluctantly retired once again under the ashes ready to rise again at the slightest whiff of carrion. Mixed or not, this metaphor accurately described how I felt about the press.

And all the while, Belinda slowly healed: first in the private sanatorium to which she was transferred and then under her brother's solicitous and nurturing care when he brought her back to his home in Brookfield.

And now Robert was dead. And this time how could it be considered a suicide? How could it be considered anything but murder? Was this all happening again? I was afraid that it was. And sadly I knew my nagging doubts about Belinda had returned. And that cracking sound I heard inside me was my heart breaking.

"Oh, Sophie," I whispered, "could she have done it?"

She paused for a moment and then said, "It would seem that the police are certainly suspicious of her."

"I'm sure of that. But what do *you* think?"

"Look, boss, I know how you feel about Belinda. I know how much both of you went through three years ago. I don't want to see you go through all that again."

"You know how much I appreciate your concern, Sophie. But I would like to know your thoughts about this. Do you think Belinda could be a killer?"

"Well," she took a deep breath and then continued, "to be perfectly honest with you, when her husband was killed, and when it came out that he was unfaithful to her, I did think it was possible that she might have found out about it somehow that night, and she might have flipped out. She might not have known what she was doing, but, yes, I did think at the time that it might have been possible that she killed Luke and then repressed the fact entirely."

"I see. And what about her brother? Do you think she could have killed him as well? Please, Sophie, tell me what you really think."

"Harry, I saw how hard Robert fought for you to hire his sister on Saturday. I then saw how Belinda reacted when she learned Robert had collapsed. I saw how she insisted that she ride in the back of the ambulance with him to the hospital. I saw how truly relieved and delighted she was when she learned he was better. It is clear in my mind that both of them loved each other unconditionally.

"I then saw her demeanor with you back at the theater that same evening and at the hospital yesterday. I saw how she had changed, how she had emotionally evolved. That's a pretty highfalutin phrase to come out of my mouth, but I mean it. Belinda is a good actress, but she's not good enough to fake that. I believe with all my heart that this is not the same Belinda we knew for years in New York, the glamorous, ambitious, passionate and, yes, very much self-involved Belinda we knew. And this is definitely not the same Belinda we saw at Bellevue. That woman might have had the pride and anger in her to strike back at a cheating husband. That woman's ego might have been so strong that such a humiliation might have totally unhinged her. It is within the realm of possibility. At least I thought it possible.

"But this woman we have seen for the last few days, this woman who has gone through such anguish, this woman who has gone through hell and come out the other side so much stronger and clearer and much more genuine, this woman could never have killed the brother she loved so much. This woman did not kill Robert no matter how bad it looks. And I'm now beginning to doubt that she could ever have had it in her to kill anyone, even a cheating husband. But much more important than how I feel about this is how you feel, Harry. Do you think it's possible that Belinda is a murderer?"

Before I could begin to formulate my thoughts, Dr. Freemount entered the hospital room. He looked exhausted.

"How's Belinda doing, Augie?" I asked.

"She's in deep shock, I'm afraid. I have to admit that I'm quite concerned. But at least one of my patients seems to have improved. You look much better, Harry."

"Thank you, Augie, I'm all right now. Have you talked with the police?"

"Yes, I'm afraid so. I don't think it's telling tales out of school to say that she seems to be in very hot water. There appears to be no doubt at all that Robert was murdered. The worker at the Shelter, her name apparently is Rory McClintock, has identified Belinda as the only other visitor who had gone to the kennel area after Robert arrived. She said she had then seen Belinda drive away in a hurry. Apparently the McClintock woman hadn't seen her return, for after you had talked with her, she followed you a few minutes later and was surprised to see Belinda back there again, this time holding the body in her arms. I can't believe that Belinda could have done such a thing. She was so devoted to her brother. But it doesn't look good."

Sophie then said exactly what I had been thinking, "It seems so unbelievable, so ironic, Doctor, that Robert appeared to be at death's door on Saturday, then through your great help was able to fully recover, only to die so violently two days later."

"It's one for the books, that's for sure," said Augie shaking his head. "Robert was such a fine man; he didn't deserve this. He had been my patient and my friend for a long time. He sure didn't deserve any of this."

"Although it's irrelevant now, I'm still not sure I understand what caused him to collapse in front of Sophie and me at the theater. I heard it involved his diabetes."

"Yes, that's right," Augie said. "Robert had gone into insulin shock. Diabetic coma is a term that's also commonly used."

"And what caused it, Augie, do you know?" I asked.

"Well, I hate to say it, but as far as I can tell it was precipitated by you, Harry, or at least by one or more of your prune Danish."

CHAPTER

21

IF I HADN'T BEEN FULLY depressed before, I certainly was by the time Augie finished his medical monologue on hypoglycemia, retinopathy, nephropathy, neuropathy, and other equally entertaining topics. The gist of it all seemed to be that although diabetics who keep their blood sugar levels down to acceptable limits lessen the risk of complications, occasionally their sugar levels fall too far. Undue stress, among many other factors, can result in such a *low*. When Robert Gregory talked to Sophie and me at the theater, he had exhibited the condition's classic symptoms: excessive sweating, confused talk, stammering, disorientation, stumbling and the like. Later, Robert had confided to Augie that he had felt light-headed in the outer lobby while waiting to see me and suspected his sugar level had dangerously dropped. So he grabbed the nearest supply of sugar he could find: the breakfast pastries I had asked Sophie to remove from my sight and take out to the lobby because of my severe gastric distress that morning.

"What he needed," Augie continued, "was about 25 mg of sugar which he could have gotten from glucose tablets he should have been carrying with him, or even some Lifesavers, or canned fruit juice. What he didn't want was something artificially sweetened or something high in fats."

"Like my damned Danish and donuts!" I wailed.

"Right. Fats will impede the rapid absorption of sugar."

So, without knowing it, I had started the chain of events that had almost killed Robert on Saturday. But my guilt did not end there. While Augie continued to drone on and on, my mind tuned him out and started streaming on its own until it reached this sad conclusion: the chain of events that I had helped to forge had indeed ultimately and inexorably led from Robert's near death on Saturday to his actual murder today.

My reasoning process went something like this:

IF:　　I had never accepted the grant to come to Brookfield in the first place, **THEN:**

☞　　Charlie would never have come here and would still be alive today,

☞　　**AND** therefore Hazel's dreams for happiness would not have been shattered,

☞　　**AND** Frank and even little Lucy would still have the friend they loved.

IF:　　Charlie had not died, **THEN:**

☞　　Lucy would never have been taken to the Animal Shelter,

☞　　**AND** Robert would never have gone there to check on her for me,

☞　　**AND** therefore Robert would never have been murdered there.

SO, THEREFORE, IF: I had never come to Brookfield, **THEN:**

☞　　Robert would not have had the need to come to the theater to plead for Belinda,

☞ **AND** therefore would not have eaten the Danish,

☞ Which led to his hospitalization,

☞ Which led two days later to his murder,

☞ **AND** Belinda's state of shock,

☞ **AND** her possible arrest for his murder,

☞ **AND...** ☞ ☞ ☞☞ ☞ ☞ ☞ ☞ ☞ ☞ ☞

There was no way to conjecture how long my mind would have swum round and round in these ever widening ripples of blame had not Sophie asked, "Harry, are you all right?" and snapped me out of it.

Both Sophie and Augie were looking at me so strangely that I could only respond with, "Sure. Just peachy. How are you?" I then quickly continued, "So, what can we do to help Belinda? Does she need a good lawyer? Does she have a good lawyer?"

Augie replied, "I believe Robert and Belinda used old Judge Griffin as their attorney."

"I don't think it would be a bad idea then to contact 'old Judge Griffin' to let him know what's happened and determine what her legal rights are. Don't you agree, Augie?"

"Yes, I do. Bertie Griffin is a longtime friend of mine as well. I'll certainly make sure that he's notified."

"Thanks, Augie. Now do you think I can get out of here? I really do feel a whole lot better. If I can survive your erudite lecture on blood glucose levels, I believe I can survive anything."

He smiled and said he'd arrange for my discharge at the desk. Shaking hands, he turned and left the room. Immediately thereafter, Sophie said, "What's with you, Harry? Are you really all right? That was the weirdest expression I've ever seen on your face, and believe me I've seen plenty."

"That expression, I cringe to reveal, my dear Sophie, was pure, unadulterated Guilt. Yes, Guilt, with a capital *gihh*! It's an emotion that's not particularly familiar to me. No wonder it looked weird to you."

"Guilt? For what?"

"Oh, nothing much, just for ultimately being responsible for every rotten thing that's happened around here. If I hadn't chosen to make this happy little journey to rural America, none of this would have happened. You have to admit that."

"I admit nothing. Harry, for a smart guy, you're acting like a jackass. You may have a high opinion of yourself, but, I hate to spring it on you, you're not God. You had no way of knowing any of this would happen. The death of Charlie (whether it was an accident or a murder as Hazel thinks) and the stabbing of Robert Gregory have, I'm glad to say, nothing to do with you. So just get over yourself, and let's get back to finding out who really were responsible for these terrible things. Okay? Okay, King Edward the Confessor?"

I had to laugh. "Okay, okay. Actually, it's more correct to call him Saint King Edward the Confessor, but let's not quibble."

"Right," Sophie rolled her eyes, "let's not quibble. Listen, I don't know about you, but I'm starving. Could we please get a bite before I fall over?"

"Sure, Sophie, why not? Where are Hazel and Frank? Maybe they can join us for a late lunch."

"They took my car after dropping me off here. There were a couple of other leads from Charlie's receipts they wanted to pursue as well. They were then planning to come back here if we hadn't contacted them first."

"Well, why don't you call Hazel and see what's doing? By the way, Sophie, I think I remember you telling me that you were able to get Charlie's package from UPS and his laptop, right?"

"Yes, indeedee, we had no problem at all. I called you right after we got them, but you had just found Belinda and I'm afraid were not making too much sense. We then rushed over to the Shelter, so we never had the chance to look at them. They're still in my car. We'll examine them when we meet up with Hazel and Frank."

With that, she called Hazel's cell phone. When the phone was answered, Sophie looked a bit taken aback and then whispered to me that it was Frank who had answered. Remembering the last time he had answered Hazel's phone, I unconsciously rubbed my still tender nose. After a few moments, Sophie hung up. There was a pensive look on her face.

"Frank answered because Hazel was a bit upset. She received a call from the funeral home informing her that Charlie's body has just been delivered there. The two of them are driving over there now to make the final arrangements. Frank wondered if we'd like to meet them there. He thinks Hazel needs all the friends around her that she can get right now. Do you think you're up to it, Harry?"

In truth, I wasn't up to it. But I told Sophie that I was. We met Augie in the hospital elevator. He of course knew that the body had been transported and wished Hazel and us well. He in fact was on his way back to Belinda's room to check in on her. As the elevator opened on the third floor and Augie got out, we could see the burly cop stationed outside her room. A shiver went up my spine.

Sophie drove us in my car to the address Frank had given her. I know we both felt a twinge of emotion when I entered the funeral home's address on the GPS. As Mandy calmly and efficiently once again directed us through the streets of Brookfield, her robotic voice was the only sound spoken.

We parked next to Sophie's Volkswagen in Mila and Son's spacious parking lot and entered the tasteful reception room of the gracious looking building. Soothing organ music could be softly heard as the decorous and considerate staff member informed us that we would find Miss Forrest in the chapel to our right. Our footsteps made no sound in the thick carpeting as we crossed to the door of the chapel and opened it without a sound.

We saw Frank sitting in the front pew next to his friend. His massive arm was gently curled around her shoulders protecting her as well as he could from what lay immediately ahead. Sophie and I slowly walked down the narrow aisle and sat in the seats directly behind them. Hearing us sit down, Hazel turned her head back to us and sadly smiled. She was just about to whisper to me when we all jumped.

A loud and insistent car horn was blaring outside the building. After waiting for it to subside for a few seconds, Frank suddenly said, "I think that's coming from the parking lot." With a strange look on his face, he quickly left the chapel. Not knowing what else to do, I followed him.

When I got outside, I saw that Frank was examining Sophie's car in the parking lot. As I ran to him, I heard what sounded like a motorcycle roaring off. When I reached Frank, he turned to me with a look of anger and muttered, "Her car's been broken into."

CHAPTER 22

FRANK THEN SAID FOUR CONSECUTIVE sentences that I shall never forget. The first and second were the informative but upsetting: "Damn, he used a slim jim to get in" and "Oh hell, he got the laptop and the UPS package." Frank's next disturbing sentence was even more successful in capturing my full attention: "I think we can still catch that bastard." Before I could respond with something like "What do you mean WE?" the fourth and undoubtedly the most startling sentence of all was already out of Frank's mouth: "Come on, get in."

And suddenly, somehow we were both inside Sophie's orange beetle. Frank was in the driver's seat, and I was beside him finding it difficult to keep the damaged passenger door shut as we lurched forward accompanied by the sound of tires screeching and gears stripping.

Think of some of the greatest car chases in action films: Steve McQueen's Ford Mustang careening through the hills of downtown San Francisco in "Bullitt" perhaps or Gene Hackman's Pontiac LeMans obsessively pursuing an elevated subway train through Bensonhurst, Brooklyn in "The French Connection." Well, they don't hold a gear shift to Harrison "Hot Shoe" Hunt and Frank "Grand Prix" Gerrardi's manic motoring through the environs of Brookfield attempting to overtake the helmeted motorcyclist who somehow managed to keep the distance ever constant between us.

All I could make out about him was that he was wearing a denim jacket and jeans and had what looked like a medium-sized parcel strapped to the back of the cycle's seat. The high speed chase was so chaotic and stressful that I can only now remember a few harrowing details. They are recorded in my brain cells like freeze frames from Hollywood's scariest shockers.

For example, when we passed a little old lady driving a gray sedan that had practically been sideswiped by the biker moments before, the motorist's panic-stricken expression far surpassed that of Janet Leigh's in the Bates Motel shower stall or Tippi Hedron's while being attacked by swooping kamikaze feathered fiends. Two other heart stopping moments I shall never forget: the way we bounced as if on a trampoline while going over a speed bump at seventy miles an hour and the unforeseen and razor sharp turn we took barely on two wheels onto a narrow dirt road. My heart raced at Olympic record speeds. I wouldn't have been surprised if the shapes of my white-knuckled fingers were permanently impressed into the dashboard I was holding onto for dear life. For dear life? Never has a cliché been so apt.

Soon I noticed that we were following our quarry exclusively through country lanes and back roads. Suddenly Frank jammed on the brakes so hard that my seat belt and I became better acquainted than I would like to reveal. I quickly noticed why Frank had stopped the car. The helmeted thief was driving his bike up a grassy hill much too steep for any car to navigate.

"I think that little road over there might parallel the hill he's climbing up," Frank then said. "Let's see if it does."

It was more a path than a road, but we managed to negotiate it until we came to the top of the steep hill and the end of the dirt path. There was no way farther we could drive. We saw a flowing body of water below us to our left. Could it have been the same creek in which Charlie had drowned?

"There he is." Frank's words made me look straight ahead. About fifty feet in front of us I saw our prey. He had evidently thought he had finally eluded us and had idled his bike to rest after his exertions. Frank shut off the car's ignition and opened the door. Hearing the sound, the biker turned and saw us. Rays of sunlight reflected off his metal helmet allowing me to see nothing of his face making him appear even more menacing and otherworldly.

I gulped. Loudly.

"What's he doing?" I asked Frank as we saw the figure reach behind himself, lift something or other above his head and throw it down toward the water to his right. With one quick and insolent wave of his hand, he turned the motorcycle in the direction he had come and drove it back down the steep hill.

"Let's see if we can recover that laptop or whatever it was he threw," Frank said as he started climbing down the other side of the hill toward the water. I followed him. It was even more difficult going down to the bottom of this hill through the wild vegetation than it had been for Sophie and me when we had followed Lucy down a similar decline on Sunday. Finally, we had descended far enough to see that the water was not directly at the bottom of the hill as it had been behind Charlie's house but a number of yards farther away.

"I think we're in luck. It probably didn't fall in the water," Frank said with a sigh of relief. We both spread out and began searching through the thick undergrowth. It was hard going, and for a time it looked as if we were not going to be successful. But all of a sudden I got lucky and spied a bit of cardboard half covered by a thicket of wild roses. Carefully trying to avoid the thorns (regrettably and rather painfully I'm afraid I was not wholly successful), I picked up the cardboard container.

"Well, it's not the laptop after all. It's the package we picked up this morning from UPS," Frank informed me. "I don't think he threw more than one object, do you?"

"It didn't look like it to me. But just to be sure let's keep going."

A half hour of fruitless searching later, we agreed that the laptop probably still remained in the biker's possession, and we slowly climbed back up the hill and got in the car. I had shaken the package as soon as I had picked it up. And I did so now once again. Unfortunately, the rattling I heard seemed to indicate that the package had been severely damaged in its fall down the hill.

"Should we open it now or wait till we get back to Hazel and Sophie?" Frank asked.

"You might have the patience of Job, but I sure as hell don't. We've gone through much too much to wait any longer before finding out what's in this damned box," I said as I tried my best to tear it open. Frank provided a handy pocket knife that easily sliced through the packing tape, and the contents of this long sought after prize were finally revealed.

After the police and ambulances arrived at the Animal Shelter, Ms. Bobbie and I were both taken to Brookfield Memorial Hospital. I was released within a few hours, but Ms. Bobbie was suffering from severe shock and remained under Dr. Freemount's watchful care. Ms. Xerxes and I then joined Ms. Forrest at the funeral home where she finalized arrangements for Mr. Wetherstone's cremation. The ceremony held late that afternoon. was mercifully short.

And surprisingly moving. I had expected that Hazel, Frank, Sophie and I would be the only witnesses to the somber ritual. I was therefore extremely pleased to see both Augie and Louise Freemount in attendance. They apparently had contacted members of the theater's board and others connected with the operation of the theater resulting in about twenty sympathetic and kindly souls filling the pews of the little chapel. Considering that none of the Brookfield residents had ever met Charlie, their support and empathy for our loss were particularly touching.

It was nice to see Joey Patowski there. She was as authentically affable as ever and said one or two things to Sophie and me that were very sweet and really very sensitive. When she quietly introduced me to her six foot six "baby brother" Bill, I could see that she was not the only member of the Patowski family to inherit a gentle and caring manner.

The other designers I had met on Sunday were also in attendance. The CPA/sound maven Ken Gleason had brought his wife Kathleen, and the exotic costumière Sylvie Darnell had brought a man she identified only as her "significant other". Both companions were totally unlike what I would have imagined. The spouse of the seemingly unassuming, rather asexual Ken oozed sensuality and gregariousness. Sylvie's friend was as reserved and conservative as she was flamboyant and flighty. All of them showed consideration and kind concern for those of us grieving, and I could see how especially helpful this was to Hazel. I now for the first time understood how beneficial "the kindness of strangers" could be. The anger and resentment I had been feeling about Brookfield dissipated a bit during the forty minute ceremony.

And then it was over. After the guests had shaken our hands, hugged our shoulders, and offered their parting words of consolation, only the Freemounts remained in the chapel with the four of us. While Augie talked quietly with Hazel and Frank in one corner, I saw that Louise was standing alone in another apparently waiting for Augie to conclude his conversation.

I left Sophie who was thanking the funeral director for his kind efficiency and walked over to Louise. She was dabbing at her eyes with a pretty little handkerchief.

"Thank you so much for coming, Louise," I said to her, "and for getting all the other people here as well."

"No one should go through a loss like this alone," she softly said. Then Augie joined us, and after a few words they were gone as well. I slowly walked back to the others who were now quietly sitting in the front pew.

"Well, it's finally over," Sophie sighed.

"I'm afraid it won't ever be really over until we find who was responsible," Hazel calmly said. "Until we identify that man on the motorcycle. Until we find out why he had been tormenting Charlie for so long. Until we find out why he sent him this despicable thing the day he killed my poor Charlie."

Hazel then reached for her bag and, as she had many times since we had shown her the package we had recovered, she once again pulled out and stared at the pieces of plastic and porcelain that had once formed the snow globe. As the tears flowed again down her cheeks, my anger suddenly returned.

CHAPTER

23

YES, IT WAS ONLY A snow globe that was in the package sent to Charlie and which caused both Frank and Hazel to become so emotional when they each first saw it. It was only a snow globe, one of those transparent spheres usually made of glass enclosing a miniature scene of some sort. The sphere which stands on a plastic base also contains liquid which serves as the medium through which the "snow", now often composed of tiny granules of white plastic, slowly falls over the scene when the globe is shaken. Many snow globes also had built in music boxes. Modern technology has allowed sound chips to substitute for the older music boxes in many cases.

Yes, it was only a snow globe. But, as Frank told me, this was the sixth one that had been sent to Charlie. Twice a year for the last three years a snow globe had been sent precisely on the eleventh of August and the eleventh of May. True to form, the UPS slip had specified this latest snow globe had been delivered on May 11th. Each one had been sent to wherever Charlie happened to be staying on those dates. And each one had been sent anonymously. There was never any card or written message included. And although each snow globe was different, each was a cruel variation on a similar theme: a movie or television scene showing the deleterious effects of alcohol abuse. Three of these "booze globes" as Charlie had called them were comic; three were dead serious.

The first one he received showed a little porcelain figure of the film comedian W.C. Fields, he of the big red nose and drunken persona, the hater of children and animals, the lover of all things alcoholic. The figure showed Fields wearing his familiar straw hat trying to maintain his balance by holding onto a lamp post. Frank remembered that the built in sound chip continuously played Fields inimitably delivering such lines from his films as: "Victoria dear, some weasel took the cork out of my lunch," "I feel as though a midget with muddy feet had been walking over my tongue all night" and "Was I in this saloon here last night, and did I spend a twenty dollar bill? Yeah? Oh, boy. What a load that is off my mind. I thought I'd lost it."

Charlie had apparently been rather amused when he had received this first snow globe since he had always been a movie buff and had been a fan of Fields. In fact, as I told Frank, I remembered going to a marathon of W.C. Fields' movies one night with Charlie when we were at Yale and then spending the rest of the night and early the next morning carousing with him and some of his drinking buddies.

Charlie was less amused the next May when he received the second snow globe, which this time immortalized the dramatic film "The Lost Weekend." The little porcelain scene depicted the tragic alcoholic played by Ray Milland sitting at a bar. When Hazel talked to me about this one, she told me Charlie and she had played the snow globe's recording from the film so many times that they could recite it by heart, and she did so for me in the funeral parlor. It went like this:

"*It shrinks my liver, doesn't it, Nat? It pickles my kidneys, yes. But what does it do to my mind? It tosses the sandbags overboard so the balloon can soar. Suddenly, I'm above the ordinary. I'm confident, supremely confident. I'm walking a tightrope over Niagara Falls. I'm one of the great ones. I'm*

Michelangelo molding the beard of Moses. I'm van Gogh painting pure
sunlight. I'm Horowitz playing the 'Emperor Concerto.' I'm John Barrymore
before the movies got him by the throat. I'm Jesse James and his two brothers.
All three of them! I'm W. Shakespeare. And out there, it's not 3rd Avenue
any longer. It's the Nile, Nat, the Nile, and down it floats the barge of
Cleopatra."

She and Charlie had agonized over who could have sent these two
globes to him and why. When the third one arrived the next August,
Charlie was reluctant even to open it. But, with Hazel's encouragement,
he of course did. This one was a seemingly benign scene from Disney's
animated film "Dumbo" showing the baby elephant and his friend
Timothy the mouse sitting in a tree drunkenly watching three gigantic
pink elephants blowing their trumpet shaped trunks. The globe played
the cartoon's related song. Hazel remembered these lyrics in particular:

> "Look out! Look out!
> Pink elephants on parade
> Here they come!
> Hippety hoppety
> They're here and there
> Pink elephants ev'rywhere
> Look out! Look out!
> They're walking around the bed
> On their head
> Clippety cloppety
>
> What'll I do? What'll I do?
> What an unusual view!
> I could stand the sight of worms
> And look at microscopic germs
> But technicolor pachyderms
> Is really much for me
> I am not the type to faint
> When things are odd or things

Are quaint
But seeing things you know that ain't
Can certainly give you an awful fright!
What a sight!
Chase 'em away!
Chase 'em away!
I'm afraid I need your aid
Pink elephants on parade!

When the next two snow globes arrived, Frank said that Charlie had told him that he was not affected by them at all, that he considered them merely a sick joke from some long lost acquaintance with a bizarre sense of humor. Hazel said that she knew, however, that each new appearance of a snow globe required extra concentration on Charlie's part to keep his equilibrium and focus. Although he continued to go to AA meetings regularly, he attended many more in May and August than he did the other months of the year.

The fourth snow globe depicted the debauched toga scene from "National Lampoon's Animal House". The miniature John Belushi was raising a bottle as his recorded voice said, "My advice to you is to start drinking heavily." To which a fraternity brother intoned, "You better listen to him, Flounder. He's in Pre-Med."

Last August, a porcelain film poster for "Days of Wine and Roses" was enclosed in the glass sphere. Tiny photos of Jack Lemmon and Lee Remick stared out at Charlie when he removed the globe from the package. Above their heads furled the words: THIS, IN ITS OWN TERRIFYING WAY, IS A LOVE STORY. Lemmon's recorded voice blazed out from the globe: "We have more than a couple of drinks. We get drunk! Then we stay drunk most of the time. Look at that dump that we live in and the clothes that we wear... We send that child off to school like she's... Look at me. I'm a drunk, and I don't do my job, and that's it!"

After this one, Charlie could no longer pretend to himself or others that he was not seriously affected by the snow globes. He was resolved to discover who was sending them to him and what the reason was behind these malicious gifts. He had gone to the police and the post office, but they had not been helpful. A few months ago, he hired a private detective who had apparently made some progress. He would not confide to anyone, not even Hazel or Frank, what had been discovered or even the name of the detective. He had emphatically stated that this was a matter only between the sender of these packages and himself. No one else, he determined, could be involved. But he had told Hazel that during the cross country trip he would be taking to come to Brookfield he hoped he would be able personally to find out the answer to this mystery and settle the matter once and for all.

Frank thought some of the receipts and notes which had out of state addresses or phone numbers as well as the Google maps which Sophie and I had found in Charlie's van might be of help in reconstructing his search. Hazel wished we had been able to maintain control of Charlie's laptop, as it had been his habit to keep a daily computer journal of his activities. She felt sure that if he had made any discoveries on his trip, he would have entered them on this journal. Still, Frank maintained that if the paper trail could be followed, we might reach some interesting conclusions.

It was seeing the sixth and latest snow globe that convinced Frank that he himself would be in the best position to ferret out these addresses. Since Charlie's cremation was concluded, he saw no benefit for either Hazel or him to stay on in Brookfield. As she wanted to take Charlie's van back with her (they had both bought the car together as their first engagement gifts to each other, and it was very special to her), they decided she would drive the van back home to Oregon herself. The time she would spend alone would be of benefit to her, she told us. She had had no time at all to think since she heard the terrible news from Dr. Freemount. Frank decided to fly to the relevant cities himself in his own plane and would keep in touch with Hazel and us each step of the way. He had our cell phone numbers, and I was sure Dr. Freemount had a fax machine that we could use if necessary. I would let him know the fax number tomorrow.

Before we left the funeral home to drive Hazel and Frank back to the Inn for their final night there, as they both determined to start on their respective journeys the next morning, we took one more look at what remained of the latest snow globe. Although the glass sphere and the plastic base had been shattered in the fall and the porcelain figure had been broken in half, it was not difficult to recognize the scene. It was from an episode of the tv sitcom *I Love Lucy* in which Lucy Ricardo was rehearsing a television commercial for a vitamin tonic which contained a high alcoholic content. The miniature redhead was holding a bottle of Vitameatavegamin in one hand and a tablespoon in the other. The sound chip had also been damaged it seemed, for when we switched the sound on, all that we heard was Lucille Ball's drunken voice repeating endlessly:

> *"Do you pop out at parties?*
> *Are you unpoopular?*
> *Vitameatavegamin contains megetables and vinerals.*
> *It's so tasty too. Just like candy!"*

"How did the bastard know?" Hazel asked. *I Love Lucy* was Charlie's all time favorite. I got him the show's theme song for his cell phone only two days before he left Portland."

We drove to the Inn in silence. As we parked, I noticed once again how little business the Inn seemed to be doing. There were only a couple of cars in the large parking lot. And, all our eyes went to it immediately, one dust covered motorcycle.

CHAPTER

24

"IT CERTAINLY LOOKS LIKE THE same one," I said to Frank as we examined the motorcycle in the Inn's parking lot.

"I agree it's the same make and model," Frank replied, "but there must be so many of them around that, without knowing the license number of the one we followed, I don't see how we could be absolutely positive."

He was right of course. The leather bag that contained the stolen snow globe and computer had been strapped behind the cycle's seat in such a manner that, whether deliberately planned or not, it had obscured the license plate.

Still, Sophie copied down this bike's license number in that ubiquitous notebook of hers. "At least it won't hurt to identify the person who owns this one," she sensibly stated.

We then left the parking lot and walked around the corner to the Inn's entrance. I held the front door open for the others and was just about to go in myself when I heard the unmistakable sound of a motorcycle revving up. I don't remember ever running as fast as I did at that moment. Panting a bit, I reached the parking lot in time to see a man now seated on the cycle we had just examined. He finished putting on his helmet then adjusted the strap and drove quickly away. The helmet looked exactly like the one that would forever be engraved on my brain cells. And underneath that helmet was Randy Williamson.

As I slowly walked back, a hundred questions swirled around in my head. Was it Randy who stole the items from Sophie's car and gave us that merry chase this afternoon? Was it Randy who had sent the snow globes for the past three years to Charlie? And, if Hazel was right and Charlie had been murdered, was it Randy who had been the cold blooded killer? And if so, the big question was, of course, why? Why would twenty-five year old Randy Williamson want to kill fifty year old Charlie Wethestone? How did Randy even know Charlie to begin with? As far as any of us knew, Charlie had never been to Brookfield before, and, at least according to what I remembered from Randy's resumé, he had grown up in Brookfield and none of his theatrical credits indicated he had ever worked outside the state. The headache I could feel beginning to throb in my right temple once again was no doubt due as much to these maddening questions as to the hunger I suddenly noticed I was experiencing.

When I entered the Inn, I saw that Hazel and Frank were at the front desk talking with the self-consciously shy young woman we had seen a few times before. Frank was advising her that he and Hazel would be checking out tomorrow morning. Sophie was seated in an armchair a few feet away.

I walked over to the front desk and said to the young woman (I believe Randy had called her Meredith), "Good evening. I wonder if Randy Williamson happens to be around now."

I saw Sophie cock her head at me as I said this. I gave her a meaningful look in return that meant to listen intently to my conversation with Meredith.

"Randy?" she replied with a slight blush, "I'm afraid you just missed him. I took over for him a few minutes ago."

"Oh, really? Did that happen to be his motorcycle I heard driving away as I came in the hotel?"

Now Hazel and Frank as well as Sophie were all paying close attention as Meredith replied, "Yes, it must have been."

"So, Randy was on the day shift at the desk, and you're taking the night shift?" I asked as nonchalantly as I could.

"Yes, that's usually our schedule. Is there something you wanted him to do for you that I could help you with, Mr. Hunt?"

"Nothing very important thank you, uh, Meredith. I just thought he could recommend a nearby restaurant where we might have dinner tonight. The dining room in the Inn is closed now, isn't that right?"

She blushed again. "Yes, I'm afraid so. The dining room is only used now for special functions like the one the Barn Theater held the other night."

"Right. Randy told us he helped serve at that one."

She smiled shyly. "We all help out around here whenever we can. I'm afraid we're rather shorthanded."

It was clear she was not comfortable with any sort of small talk. Nevertheless I pressed forward. "It does seem that you folks work very long hours. I don't know how you do it. I hope you get a little time off when you're doing your long shifts. You know, time to take a lunch or dinner break or," and I giggled a little, "powder your nose."

Meredith was obviously not happy discussing her potty breaks. She softly said, "When we need to leave the desk, usually we ask the manager Mr. Higgins to relieve us."

I felt bad for the way her face turned bright pink after she realized how inappropriate the word 'relieve' was in this context, but I added, "Then, Mr. Higgins probably would have taken over for Randy today so that he could go on his meal break, I assume."

"Yes, I would suppose so." In an attempt to curtail our little talk that was obviously painful for her, she handed me a sheet of paper. "This is a list of nearby restaurants that we give out to guests at the Inn. Perhaps it will be of help to you. I usually don't go out too often, so I'm afraid I can't personally vouch for any of them."

Revealing this little bit about her personal life was evidently so difficult for her that I just thanked her politely for the list and motioned for Sophie, Hazel and Frank to follow me into the empty sitting room adjacent to the front lobby.

"So, *Randy* owns the motorcycle that we saw outside," Sophie said excitedly as we sat down in the sitting room.

"Not only that, but he wears a helmet exactly like the one worn by our friend this afternoon. I saw him put it on outside just now before he rode off into the night. And, although he seemed to have an alibi for his whereabouts this afternoon, we just heard that he probably would have been relieved by the manager during his meal break. He then could have had the time to steal the objects from Sophie's car, lead Frank and me to hell and back and return to the Inn by the end of his break. The whole chase took no more than forty minutes."

"We certainly could verify with the manager if and when he left for dinner and returned. I think we should do that right now," said Sophie.

"Wait a minute, we can always do that later," Frank interjected. "Even if he were away from his job at the Inn during the time in question, how can we prove that he indeed was the thief? Our evidence is only circumstantial I'm afraid. I think it would make more sense not to let Randy know that we're suspicious of him in any way. Not until we find more incriminating evidence. If and when we find more, then we'll most assuredly go to the cops with such an air tight case that the creep, whether it's Randy or someone else, won't be able to wriggle out of it. You told us, Harry, that you were seriously thinking of casting Randy in your plays."

"I was, but how could I now? How could I look him in the face, work with him, while all the time thinking that he may very well be Charlie's tormentor and possible killer?"

"I think, Harry, that you should cast him," Frank said. "That way, we'll always know where he is and maybe you'll be able to find more proof, more substantial proof than we have now while he's with you during the rehearsal process. Or at least keep him under observation until I check out all the addresses and phone numbers you and Sophie found in Charlie's car. What do you say?"

When I hesitated, Hazel then spoke. "I know it will be hard for you, Harry. I myself would like nothing better than to wring that murderer's neck myself. But only when I'm absolutely sure who he is. Let's do all we can until we have conclusive proof of the killer's identity. Frank will do his best to find that proof by following the route Charlie took getting here, and you and Sophie can be in an exceptionally valuable position to find out more by watching Randy's every move in rehearsal. I would be very grateful to you two if you would do that. But it's your choice, and I'm afraid it could be a dangerous choice, if Randy is indeed a killer. What do you two say?"

What could we say? Even though I knew that continually lying to someone, spying on someone, trying to entrap someone, even if that person were a possible murderer, did not sit right with me. And I knew that it would be even more difficult for Sophie, forthright, straight-shooting Sophie. What could we say? Of course we said we would.

All four of us tried to lighten our collective mood at dinner. After all, it was the last night we would be seeing Hazel and Frank for a while at least. In fact we selected the restaurant from the list given us as a tribute to our new ally Frank Gerrardi. It was a cute little bistro named *Franks' Place*. No, that wasn't a typo. The name was meant to be a possessive plural. The owner of the restaurant was apparently named

Frank something or other. So the theme he selected for the décor and menu was famous namesakes of his. There were posters and paintings throughout the restaurant of such notable Franks as Franklin Delano Roosevelt, Frankie Lane, St. Francis of Assisi, and on and on. The bill of fare included such dishes as the Frankenstein Fried Chicken, the Frank Zappa Ziti, the Francis Coppola Compote and the Frankie Valli Chili with Four Season(ing)s.

I was really beginning to enjoy myself until the waiter arrived to take our orders. He was wearing an apron that was emblazoned with the face of old blue eyes himself. Suddenly, the content of the nightmare I had experienced while being sedated by Dr. Freemount came back to me once again in its entirety. In a flashing moment I once again saw the vaguely familiar Lady Macbeth hand me the three torn pieces of paper. As the three words once again flashed in front of me:

their meaning suddenly became clear. For some reason, my subconscious had dredged up some of the lyrics to an old Frank Sinatra song I hadn't thought of in years. I think I remembered that it came out in the sixties. I could hear Sinatra singing it now in my mind.

> *Let's take it nice 'n' easy*
> *It's gonna be so easy*
> *For us to fall in love*
>
> *Hey baby what's your hurry*
> *Relax and don't you worry*
> *We're gonna fall in love*

We're on the ROAD to romance - that's safe to say,
But let's make all the stops along the way.

The PROBLEM now of course is
To simply hold your horses
To rush would be a CRIME
'Cause nice 'n' easy does it every time

But, the problem now of course was: why, for heaven's sake, had I thought of the song *Nice 'N' Easy* during my dream? For the life of me, I hadn't a clue.

CHAPTER
25

ONE WOULD THINK THAT AFTER a day like today, food would be the farthest thing from my mind. However, I must admit that savoring the *Frankly* flavorful fare at the theme restaurant did help to take my mind away from recent calamities for an hour or two at least. It wasn't until I swallowed the final blissful bite of my Frank Perdue Prodigious Profiterole that I made the call to Augie Freemount. He had told us that he would be returning to the hospital directly from the funeral home to check on Belinda's condition.

"No good news to report I surmise," Sophie softly said after looking at my face as I put down the cell phone.

"No, I'm afraid not. Belinda is still in acute shock. Augie sounded even more worried than before."

"Oh, Harry, I'm so sorry. This waiting must be agony for you." And this concern coming from someone who really knew what agony was! Quite a woman this Hazel Forrest was proving herself to be.

"Well, at least we can do more than just sit around and wait in regard to our other problem," I said trying to sound more positive. At dinner the four of us had worked out a plan of action for tomorrow. Bright and early, I would drive Hazel to the Animal Shelter. There had never been a doubt in her mind that she would take Lucy back home with her to Oregon. Throughout the time we had spent with Hazel, she had often talked about Charlie's little dog, about how concerned she was about her, about Lucy's sweet nature and devotion to her master. It was obvious to the rest of us that being together would be the best thing in the world for both of "Charlie's Angels." When Frank had revealed at dinner that this was the term Charlie had used to describe his two favorite females, Hazel's eyes had not been the only ones glistening.

And so we bade good night once again to our two new friends at the front entrance of the Inn. We could barely make out mousey Meredith at the reception desk self-consciously smiling at them as they crossed the lobby.

As Sophie and I drove back to Pemberley Cottage, I told her about the weird dream I had suddenly remembered at dinner. When I mentioned that the song "Nice 'N' Easy" apparently figured strongly in it, she gave me a strange look.

"Why does that song crooned by Sinatra, or, no, by two Sinatra look-alikes, ring a bell for me? It's connected with some show done years ago at Yale Drama, I'm sure of it."

"Wait a minute!" I exclaimed. "You're absolutely right. A parody of that song *was* used in one of the musical revues our class put on that spoofed the school and New Haven, that sort of thing. My Lord, I haven't thought of that show for decades. You've got the memory of an elephant, Sophie. So what made me think of it now? And what does it have to do with Belinda and the deaths of her husband and brother? I didn't meet Belinda until years after I left Yale."

"It probably doesn't really have anything to do with anything. You know how crazy dreams can be. You directed that show, didn't you? You took charge of all the revues staged the years you were there."

"Yes indeed. Those shows and their success helped me get a foothold in the business."

"Everyone in your class would have contributed to those revues, right? So can you remember what Charlie's connection was to this one? Did he design the sets?"

"I think he did. But he probably also added to the script and song lyrics. Everyone did. I'm afraid I only have a vague recollection of the details of the show. Too bad that was way before video recorders were around. I would love to look at that show today to see if it was half as good as the reviewers said."

"Yale might still have copies of the program and maybe even the script and music. They usually kept records of every show held at the school."

"Do you think so, Sophie? Whether or not it can help us in our sleuthing, I really would like to see what's available."

"All I can do is try." Sophie then and there took out her cell phone and little notebook and text messaged someone. (That's what this astounding procedure is called, I believe.) When she finished she explained that she had sent a message to her old friend Madge Magill who was the current head librarian and keeper of the archives at Yale Drama School.

"If anyone can find that material, it's Madge. And she owes me a favor or two. I included Dr. Freemount's fax number. We'll see what she comes up with."

Have I mentioned how happy I am that Sophie is in my life?

When we arrived at Pemberley Cottage, Augie was still up enjoying a late night cup of cocoa in the kitchen. We gladly accepted his offer to join him. We kept our voices down as Louise had already gone to bed. Augie told me that the police had been around earlier and had requested that I go down to the station at my earliest convenience to discuss what I had witnessed at the Animal Shelter that afternoon.

"If only I could make them believe that Belinda could never have murdered Robert," I said to Augie.

"I certainly wish you the best of luck, Harry. But they seem pretty steadfast in their conviction."

On that unintentionally ominous note evoked by the double meaning of Augie's final word, we all went upstairs. It seemed as if my head had just hit the pillow when that blasted Brandenburg Concerto alerted me that it was now seven a.m. Tuesday morning. Luckily no Shakespearean related dreams had disturbed my slumber (at least none that I could remember) and I felt fairly refreshed as I performed my morning toilette and met Sophie in the kitchen a scant twenty minutes later. Louise had prepared a lovely breakfast for us but had barely time to say good morning to me as she and Augie left to drive separately to their workplaces: he to the hospital; she to the Pilates studio she runs.

When Sophie and I were alone in the kitchen enjoying Louise's delectable French toast, I asked her if her suspicions regarding the Freemounts had at all changed.

"I still believe they're very worried about something that they're being very secretive about," Sophie replied, "but I must say that I do believe they're both fine people who have treated us very nicely. I only wish they'd come clean and let us know what's bothering them so much. Maybe we could help them."

"Before we can consider adding the Freemounts to our list of people to assist, today we have a lot to do for Hazel and Frank. We're scheduled to meet them at the Inn at eight. And then we both have a hell of a lot to do before the callback auditions begin at six this evening."

"When you're right, you're right," Sophie responded. "So I suggest you refrain from taking that third helping of toast you've been eyeing, and let's skedaddle."

And skedaddle we did. We took both cars to the Inn where Hazel and Frank were waiting for us outside. We then regrouped as planned. Sophie was to drive Frank to the airport where he would see to the refueling of his private plane. Sophie would keep in touch with me about his progress, as Hazel and I wanted to meet them later at the airport to see Frank off.

As Sophie and Frank headed out, Hazel got into my car and, with Mandy once again efficiently guiding us, we drove toward the Animal Shelter. We made one quick stop on the way for Hazel to pick up a coffee and roll and, bizarrely, as Lawrence Peter Berra had once observed, it was "like *déjà vu* all over again."

The early morning breakfast crowd had filled *Meals* coffee shop. The amply bosomed waitress named Dawn took Hazel's order. And once again all eyes were on me. And once again those eyes watched me as I picked up a copy of the newly delivered morning edition of the *Brookfield Bugle*. And once again I saw that damned unflattering picture of me on the front page. Only this time it was not alone.

This time, two other photos were positioned next to mine gruesomely jockeying for attention. One was a frightening shot of Lucy standing in a corner of the Shelter's exercise area snarling belligerently at the camera. The other depicted a wild-eyed Belinda forcibly resisting two uniformed policemen trying to lift her from the corpse of her brother. It was either a random shaft of sunlight or the result of the photographer's flash bulb that made the knife protruding from Robert Gregory's chest appear to glow with a grotesque, supernatural brilliance.

CHAPTER

26

"HOW COULD ANYONE BE SO spiteful, so vindictive?" Hazel was fuming as she tossed the newspaper on top of the dashboard. We had made a beeline from the coffee shop as soon as we saw the *Bugle's* front page headline and were now safely back in the car and on our way.

"What does this Damian Devoe have against you? Do you even know him?"

"Never set eyes on the man nor heard of him before yesterday. But I've been told he was a vanquished competitor for the theatre position given to me this summer. That might have a little something to do with the vehemence of his venom."

"Evidently. So much for a journalist's search for the truth."

"As Mark Twain said, my dear Hazel: 'Get your facts first, and then you can distort 'em as much as you please.'"

"You're certainly viewing all this rubbish with a healthy perspective, Harry."

"Sometimes I astonish even myself," I said with a wry smile. "Ye gods, Hazel, so many terrible things have befallen all of us in such a short period of time, that if I reacted to each one with the level of invective it deserved, I'd be lying in a hospital bed next to Belinda, and that wouldn't do any of us any good, now would it? And so, I've decided to cloak myself with the serenity of Buddah." I then took a short dramatic pause before I added, "And if you believe that one, I have a bridge in Brooklyn you might be interested in."

It was nice to see Hazel smile, even if at that exact moment we passed *The Green Parrot*, and I could hear in my head once again how tormented Belinda's voice had sounded when she had called me from there.

A few minutes later, we reached the Animal Shelter and entered its office/thrift shop. The fiery red haired Rory McClintock was ensconced at the front table attending now to three rather fluffy cats. She greeted me with an odd look and quickly reminded me of my previous acquaintance with the diabetic Rhoda and then introduced both of us to the rather sleepy looking Lion and Grapefruit who had evidently through considerable practice managed to secure prime positions along with "brave little Rhoda" in the comfortable confines of Rory's considerable lap.

As Hazel had spoken to Rory on the phone yesterday about her wish to adopt Lucy, I left her there to complete the paperwork. *The Green Parrot* was still on my mind, and I had decided to pop over there for a few minutes now just on the off chance that I could ferret out more information. I told Hazel of my plan and said I should be back to collect her and Lucy in a half hour or so. As I turned to leave the thrift shop, I saw the reason why Rory had given me that odd look a few minutes before. The morning edition of the *Bugle* was lying on the very edge of the table apparently where Rory had pushed it when we had entered. It was heartening to see how quickly news spread in this information age. Inquiring minds certainly want to know, *don't you know?*

The Green Parrot seemed entirely different at nine in the morning from the way it had yesterday at noontime. There was no loud rock music blasting this time. In fact, the bar and grill was strangely quiet and empty. The only sound I heard as I entered was the sibilant swish of the cleaning woman's mop washing the barroom's floor. Her back was to me as I said, "Hello. I'm sorry to disturb you, but is Joe Flaherty around?"

Apparently the woman was so absorbed in her work that she paid no attention to what I said and offered no reply. I politely cleared my throat. Again there was no response. A little confused, I walked a few steps closer to her and once again said, "Excuse me. Could you help me?" Nada. A little annoyed, I was about to go up to her and tap her on the shoulder, when she calmly and efficiently picked up her bucket and turned in my direction. It would be an impossible task to determine which one of us was then more startled: the middle aged woman, as she spotted me for the first time and loudly screamed, or I, as I physically jumped and audibly gasped at her totally unexpected and shrill shriek.

We both simultaneously said, "Sorry." And then as she asked, "Can I help you?" I could see by the way her eyes focused on my lips awaiting my answer that she was deaf.

"Yes, thank you. I wonder if Joe Flaherty is here."

"No, he isn't." I could see she was an expert lip reader. "No one else but me comes in before ten," she continued. "I know you, don't I? You're that Mr. Hunt from New York, aren't you?"

"Yes, I am." I could feel my hackles (whatever they are) rise. "I presume you're another dedicated and devoted reader of the ever fair and balanced *Brookfield Bugle*," I said in a rather sarcastic tone.

"Actually, I'm not," she replied with a smile. "I never give that scandal sheet the time of day. No, it was my sister-in-law Joey who told me all about you when she came in here for a drink yesterday just after you left. I'm Anna Patowski, Bill's wife. And we're all as sorry as we could be about what's happened to you and your friends the last few days."

I gratefully and rather ashamedly shook Anna's outstretched hand. "Thank you very much. You say you were here yesterday?"

"That's right. I work days. Cleaning up before the place opens and then waiting on tables for the lunch time crowd."

"Did you happen to see the actress Belinda Bobbie when she was here?"

Her face darkened as she said, "Yes, I did. The poor woman was in a terrible state. She's a friend of yours I understand."

"Yes, she is. And she's in a lot of trouble right now. I'm trying to help her, so I'd appreciate you telling me all that you saw."

"I'd be glad to, Mr. Hunt. Both Joey and my Bill have nothing but good things to say about you. Let's see now. I must have been in the kitchen when she came in, because when I first saw her she was already seated at a small table, in fact that one other there in the corner."

I looked over to where Anna had pointed. The table which was next to a window was partially hidden by a large standing birdcage occupied by an oversized wooden parrot painted a bright Kelly green."

"She looked very upset. I remember she was frantically trying to find something in her purse. She ended up dumping everything onto the table until she found her cell phone. I noticed that her keys and I think a compact had fallen onto the floor, so I went over and picked them up and handed them to her. She barely noticed me. She was so intent on trying to call someone. So, I put all the items that had fallen out of her purse back in it for her and asked her if she needed any help. I guess she didn't hear me, either because she was so upset or because of the music that people tell me is played so high in here, or maybe both. So she didn't answer me, but all the time she kept talking to herself. I tried to read her lips, but it was hard to do because she kept twisting her head back and forth. But I could make out a few words and they so troubled me that I went over to Joe, the bartender, and asked him to see if he could help. I saw him take the phone from her and walk over to a spot that was a little quieter and say a few words. So she must have reached someone before she handed the phone to Joe."

"Yes, Belinda called *me*, but I couldn't make out much of what she said because of all the music and background noise. Then what happened?"

"Since Joe was handling the matter, I went back to pick up orders in the kitchen, but before I did, I saw Belinda look out the window next to her. She looked like she saw something that terrified her and said something really weird. When I came back from the kitchen a few minutes later, Joe told me that she had vanished and asked me to check the ladies' room. She wasn't there."

"Poor Belinda. You said you were able to understand some of the words she said to herself at the table?"

"Yeah, but they seemed to make no sense, just babbling"

"What did she say? Please."

"She said several words and phrases over and over. I remember she said 'blood' and 'Robert' a number of times…"

"Right. She said those words to me on the phone."

"And she said words that looked like: 'twin', 'evil twin', and I think 'hooded twin'. And later when she saw whatever it was out the window, I'm sure the poor woman said the words 'evil twin' again and then the word 'motorcycle'."

CHAPTER

27

"*MOTORCYCLE?*" SOPHIE QUESTIONINGLY REPEATED ON the phone. "What did Belinda mean by that? And what's this *evil twin* business all about?"

"Your guess is as good as mine, I'm afraid, Sophie. Those are the words Anna Patowski thought she lip read. What they mean is another matter."

"If they mean anything at all. Poor Belinda must have been really out of it when she said those words, *if* she actually did say them." Sophie paused for a moment. "And *motorcycle?* What are we supposed to make out of that? That Belinda saw *Randy* driving his motorcycle outside the bar's window? That *Randy* is somehow this crazy evil twin? That *Randy* is somehow mixed up in Robert Gregory's death as well as in Charlie's? Now I'm getting one of your famous headaches."

"You of all people better hold yourself together till we get to the bottom of all this. I'm almost back at the Animal Shelter. I'll pick up Hazel and Lucy, and we'll meet you at the airport."

"Okay. Frank should be ready to take off by then. While we're waiting for you, I'll tell him what Belinda supposedly said at *The Green Parrot*. Maybe he can make some sense out of it."

"Maybe he can. I hope so. See you soon, Sophie." I hung up and had just parked the car when I saw Hazel walking towards me holding Lucy on a smart new leash. Both of then looked one hundred percent better than they had when I last saw them. It was obvious how good they were for each other. As she waited for me to join them, Hazel bent down and patted little Lucy who instantly responded by licking Hazel's smiling face so fast that she seemed to be contending for the Guinness World's Record for greatest number of licks given by a delighted dog to its delighted new owner.

"Well, you certainly have done wonders for Lucy. The last time I saw her she was huddling in a corner chewing on her paw near a pool of blood."

"Thank goodness, it wasn't her blood," Hazel said. "Rory couldn't wait to tell me all the grisly details. Some she learned from the police; others she read in today's paper; the rest she seems to have deduced all by herself."

"I don't doubt it. What did she say?"

While we drove to the Brookfield airport, Hazel repeated the story that Rory had so relished recounting. When the reporters and newspaper photographer had arrived at the Shelter, they created such a "hubbub" as Rory put it, that she took Lucy from the general dog population to the larger exercise area in the back. At least there the commotion wouldn't upset the other animals. Rory had then gone back to the office/thrift shop and had heard the cars of the reporters start up as they left the Shelter about fifteen minutes later.

She was sure no one else had arrived until Robert Gregory entered the office a little while later and asked to see Lucy. Rory had tried to discourage him but he told her that he had promised he would personally check on how Lucy was doing and insisted on seeing her. Since Rory knew that Robert was a frequent volunteer at the Shelter, she relented and told him that Lucy was in the exercise area.

It was then time for Rory to see about some of her other charges. She went to the barn to look after a horse there who was recovering from a former owner's abuse. All was quiet for about a quarter of an hour more until Belinda had appeared at the barn asking for her brother's whereabouts. Rory was engrossed with changing the dressings on the foal and Belinda seemed to be as insistent as her brother had been, so she told Belinda where Robert had gone. Rory was just leaving the barn to find the diabetic Rhoda when she was surprised to see Belinda hurriedly run back to her car and take off "like a bat out of you know where, honey. I sure smelled something fishy, don't you know?" Then Rory found the cat and took her back to the office to give her a shot when she met me there. When I "very rudely" ran off, she decided a few minutes later to follow me and see "just what the Sam Hill was going on." She eventually came upon me standing in front of Belinda and Robert on the ground. "Those two were positioned just like that Italian statue that made such an impression on me when I saw it at the World's Fair in New York City a while back," she had told Hazel. She had then started to talk about "how big that Big Apple was" when Hazel somehow managed to divert the conversation back to yesterday's events.

Rory was convinced that after the newspaper people had left, she had seen no one else but Robert, Belinda and me at the Shelter. She was sure that Belinda had been the only person who could have stabbed Robert. Hadn't she run away as quickly as she could, hoping that there were no witnesses to the murder? "But I saw her try to escape. Nobody can deny that. No sirree." And she had further conclusive proof of Belinda's guilt as well: "Everybody knows that a criminal always returns to the scene of the crime, don't you know? And it's common knowledge that she whacked off her poor husband in that New York City. Did I tell you how big that Big Apple was?"

"I'm sorry you had to listen to all that, Hazel."

"Me too," she laughed. "Oh, she also added that she was able to locate the three of you by using her 'good old Girl Scout training' and following the trail of blood."

She had postulated that it was Robert Gregory's blood and it had led her to his body and, she was sure, to his killer. "Shershie the fem! When in doubt, always shershie the fem!" she had told Hazel in her fractured but emphatic Franglaise and was about to embark once again on her feelings about young gals in our society today when I had arrived, and Hazel had gratefully been able to lead Lucy away to meet me.

"So what's all this about an evil twin? Apparently no one else was around," I wondered aloud. In response to Hazel's questioning look, I explained about Belinda's reported ravings at the bar and grill and had just finished when we pulled up at the tiny airport. We were able to walk Lucy over to Hanger B which now certainly appeared much less menacing than it had at five in the morning. When Lucy laid happy eyes on Frank and had received one of his fondly remembered tummy rubs, all five of us were undoubtedly all smiles. I never knew dogs could smile or had dimples. Lucy was a winner, that's for sure. A sweet tempered and loving winner. I felt absolutely certain that she would live a good life with Hazel in Oregon with frequent visits from Frank. Charlie would have been relieved.

Frank's plane was ready for take off. He told us the names of the three places he planned to visit in three different stops today before finally returning to Portland tonight. He would keep us abreast of his findings by phone and, if needed, by fax. While Hazel had a few minutes alone with Frank, I was able to read the *Bugle*'s front page editorial which Sophie had handed to me with the sourest expression I had ever seen on her face. I had only looked at the headline at the coffee shop; that had been more than enough for me at the time. If I had not been so happy for Lucy at this moment, my blood would have boiled after reading this:

DEATH TAKES NO HOLIDAY IN BROOKFIELD

An editorial by Damian Devoe

I hate to say 'I told you so.' I hate to, but I'm afraid I must. As I concluded my editorial in yesterday morning's *Bugle*, I asked what other tragic happenings might occur in Brookfield following the alcohol induced drowning of one member of the entourage of visiting New York director Harrison Hunt. I never dreamed that the answer to this rhetorical question would be provided so quickly and so horrifically.

It was the notorious Mr. Hunt himself who discovered the bloodied corpse of his crony Charles Henry Wetherstone in Brookfield Creek late Sunday afternoon.

Shockingly, it was Harrison Hunt who also happened to find a second brutalized body early the next afternoon. But this time, the tragic victim was not another New York City interloper. This time, the lifeless body was that of a well known and well liked Brookfield resident.

Robert James Gregory of 11 Sanford Road was discovered by Harrison Hunt behind an outbuilding of the Brookfield County Animal Shelter. Mr. Gregory had been brutally stabbed in the chest. And whom apparently did the unlucky Harrison Hunt happen to find holding the bleeding body to her well known and well noted bosom? No one other than the once fabled and now faded Broadway beauty, Mr. Gregory's own sister Belinda Bobbie.

Some of you may remember that Ms. Bobbie was implicated in the unsolved murder of her husband the wealthy industrialist Luke Halpert three years ago.

Some of you may remember that Mr. Halpert had been stabbed in the chest in a similar manner as Mr. Gregory. Some of you may remember that the murder weapon was a kitchen knife similar to the one found sticking out of the chest of Mr. Gregory.

Some of you may remember that Belinda Bobbie and Harrison Hunt had worked together in a number of notorious productions on and off the Great White Way. Some of you may remember that Belinda Bobbie and Harrison Hunt had in the past also been linked together romantically.

Some of you may remember that out of the kindness of his heart, Robert Gregory had taken Belinda Bobbie into his home to provide care and nurture after the unfortunate Ms. Bobbie was released from a mental hospital to which she had been institutionalized.

Some of you may think it odd that only a few days after arriving in Brookfield to assume directorial duties at the Brookfield Players' Barn Theater, Harrison Hunt happened to come across his former "good friend" Belinda Bobbie clasping the deceased body of her loving and devoted brother and only one day after finding the body of his other "good friend" Charles Henry Wetherstone.

The late Mr. Wetherstone's dog had been placed at this very same Animal Shelter after its master's dead body had been discovered. You will note exclusive photographs of the poor animal and the tragic Robert Gregory and his deranged sister as well as all the details of these brutal deaths written by this paper's star reporter in this special edition of the *Bugle*.

Welcome to Brookfield, Mr. Hunt. I hate to make any more predictions of what or whom you might come across tomorrow, or the next day, or the next.

I hate to make any more predictions. They tragically seem to come true.

I looked forward to meeting the eminent Mr. Devoe and letting him know just what I thought about him and his paper. But now, watching Frank's plane grow smaller and smaller in the sky, it was time for Hazel to finish all that she had to do before beginning her long drive back home with Lucy. She still had to check out of the Inn, and then we would all go back to Charlie's bungalow, help Hazel pack up his belongings into his van and see "Charlie's Angels" off.

I was thinking of Belinda and Charlie and what might have been, as Sophie and I separately drove the two cars once again into the Inn's parking lot. No sooner had we parked than Lucy, who along with Hazel had been riding with me, began whimpering and then suddenly began growling. When she was let out of the car, she sprang forward and sprinted to the other side of the lot. We quickly followed her, and Hazel snapped on her leash just in time as we saw at what she was snarling. It was Randy's parked motorcycle.

After sniffing both sides of the bike while continuing growling, Lucy then lurched toward the back door of the Inn and began loudly barking. We three followed closely behind. Since Hazel was having a difficult time holding onto the leash, she handed it to me, and I held it firmly in check pulling Lucy back a bit from the door at which she had begun frantically scratching. This allowed Sophie to open the back door and hold it for us. It was all I could do to keep Lucy from bounding instantly inside. I was astonished at the ferocity the previously gentle dog was suddenly displaying. Still pulling back on the leash I stepped slowly forward allowing Lucy to enter the Inn but only a few steps at a time.

We slowly passed down a short corridor and entered a little office. In the office, Lucy's growling grew louder and her sniffing grew more intense, and as Sophie opened the door at the other side of the room, Lucy let out a howl. I almost lost control of the leash as the astonished Randy heard the howling and, turning around from the reception desk in our direction, saw the maddened Lucy bare her fangs at him.

CHAPTER
28

SO MUCH THEN HAPPENED SO quickly. Randy shouted one or two rather choice expletives and backed up into a bronze magazine rack that crashed over with the sound of an exploding cannon. Lucy howled now with an ear-splitting intensity clearly in the painful 137-140 decibel range (a fact I once had learned for some strange reason that was now inconveniently flashing through my consciousness) and tried to lunge forward. I counterbalanced Lucy's lunge by pulling back on her leash with such force that my right shoulder came close to dislocating (it's still rather sore to this day). And finally with the assistance of Sophie, Hazel and even Mr. Higgins the manager who had been discussing in the nearby sitting room the details of a banquet dinner to be held in the Inn that evening with Meredith the usually shy night receptionist now apparently overcome by hysteria (judging from the ghastly shrieking we could hear emanating from the sitting room where she remained terrified by these cacophonous events in the lobby), we managed to remove Lucy from the Inn and into the secure confines of the back seat of Sophie's orange Volkswagen.

Sophie remained with Lucy and managed to quiet her down while Hazel hastened to her room and finished packing. A few minutes later she returned suitcase in hand just as I had concluded apologizing for the seventeenth time for the unfortunate disturbance in the lobby to Mr. Higgins (who turned out to be a rather pleasant *albeit* bland baby boomer), to Meredith (who cautiously had reentered the reception area now that the 'Hound of the Baskervilles', or so Lucy had seemed to this easily frightened young woman, had been safely removed) and especially to Randy (who seemed to have regained his equanimity rather quickly after Lucy had been whisked off to her pumpkin coach). Even I could see that Randy was using this opportunity to suck up to me even more than usual as he jokingly alluded to the callbacks scheduled for this evening as the perfect occasion where I could "make it all up" to him. Everyone chuckled a bit at his witticisms (I gave a Tony-winning performance at chuckling.), and bidding farewell to all, Hazel and I removed ourselves to the parking lot.

"Well, that seems to clinch it," Sophie said with a glint in her eye as we joined her in the car. "Lucy certainly recognized the motorcycle and Randy and let us and everyone else within twenty miles know how she felt about them."

"So, do you think Lucy was telling us that it was Randy who locked her in the bungalow while he did whatever it was he did that caused Charlie's death?" Hazel asked quietly.

Sophie replied, "Perhaps so. Or perhaps she recognized the bike and Randy from the Animal Shelter where she was so traumatized. Remember Belinda's mysterious evil twin, whatever that means."

"Or perhaps both," I said. "But once again, Lucy's recognition of the motorcycle and antipathy to Randy are only additional circumstantial evidence. We need more than that to put this young man behind bars. But, Hazel, don't you worry. With the information I'm sure Frank will unearth added to the sleuthing skills of Ms. Xerxes and myself, we'll find what we need and see to it that the guilty party gets what's coming to him."

With an "I hope so, Harry," Hazel holding a much calmer Lucy in her lap drove off with Sophie to Charlie's bungalow to perform the unpleasant task of packing up the van. I was to meet them there as soon as I could. However, I had another unpleasant chore to perform myself before then. Sophie had reminded me at the airport that the Brookfield police had requested my presence at the station house, how had Augie put it? oh yes, "at my earliest convenience." Now seemed as good (or more likely as bad) a time as any to make my appearance, so, with Mandy's assistance, I drove there and hoped the experience wouldn't be too onerous.

Strangely enough, it wasn't. The impression that I had formed of the local police when I had met them at the creek after finding Charlie's body and then at the hospital that evening remained intact. They were considerate of my time and feelings. Not at all the picture of the "fuzz" I had in my mind from the '60s onwards. There were no third degree interrogations, no 'good cop/bad cop" psychological ploys. Rather the meeting was efficiently and politely conducted. They even apologized for the "over the top" editorials in the daily paper. They asked me "if I wouldn't mind" writing down all relevant information concerning the two deaths and bringing it back to them in a few days. They had learned from experience that when one takes the time to put one's recollections in writing, those memories are expressed more clearly and accurately. I was in and out of the attractively decorated station quickly after having declined, would you believe, a fresh cup of tea. Although relieved, I found I was strangely disappointed at how seemingly uninterested in me they appeared to be. Apparently it had never occurred to them to think for even a fraction of a moment that I could have been more than an insignificant, unimportant, routine and rather minor player in their investigation. I was rather offended.

However, they did reveal to me rather offhandedly in passing one reason why they were certain that Robert Gregory was not a suicide but was clearly a murder victim. He had been stabbed twice. First in the left leg and then in the chest. And by their manner they seemed to be convinced that no one but Belinda had done the stabbing.

Therefore, it was with a heavy heart that I left the police discussing whether they should go to "that new French place" for lunch and followed Mandy's always expert directions back to Charlie's house.

I parked next to the mailbox where Sophie and I had found the now unneeded wedding invitations. I didn't relish climbing once more up the path to the bungalow. Luckily I didn't have to, as immediately I saw the van and Sophie's car drive down to park beside me.

All of us were in a sober mood as thoughts of what had happened here swept through our minds. Lucy was quiet and snuggled next to Hazel seeking the warmth and protection she obviously craved. The sadness and solemnity of the moment gripped each one of us, and we all were silent for several minutes, until Sophie broke the stillness and tension with a mock trumpet call and shouted: "Wagons Roll!" We laughed, kissed Hazel and Lucy goodbye, waved at the departing van till it was out of sight and then looked at each other. Sophie kindly wiped something off my cheek and then ruffled what was left of my hair. Have I mentioned how grateful I am that Sophie is in my life?

Sophie and I then decided to drive back in our two cars to Pemberley Cottage for a little lunch and a little rest before we had to leave for the theater. We would also discuss the preparations for the callback auditions. We already knew that I would cast Randy in order to keep a watch on that tricky devil (or as Sophie called him: that piece of scum) each day of rehearsals. I had also planned on casting Belinda as well. But now that was no longer a sure thing by any means. First of all, who knew whether or not she would be physically able to act this summer, and, second, would she be physically free to do so? Or, heaven forbid, would she be in police custody?

Pemberley Cottage looked like a serene haven from my tortured thoughts as we pulled up in front of its elegant front porch. Despite their bizarre reactions regarding what we were now calling Louise's un-birthday card, the Freemounts had opened their home and hearts to us. I was looking forward to spending some quality quiet time alone with Sophie in their lovely house.

As we crossed the spacious foyer, I heard a mechanical sound coming from Augie's study. I told Sophie I'd check that out as she headed into the kitchen to see about lunch. In the book lined, dark paneled study, I saw a page of paper being printed by the fax machine on the corner table. The page dropped into the receiving basket, as the machine with a jaunty beep turned itself off. I thought it must be a report from Frank but was thinking how odd that was since he had only taken off a few hours ago. There were scores of newly printed fax sheets in the basket that had been printed in reverse order so that the cover page was on top. The curtains in the study had been drawn and it was a little dark to read. I crossed to the window, drew open the curtains and now could see that the lengthy fax was addressed to Sophie from Madge Magill, her friend from Yale.

There was a notation in large bold letters on the cover sheet that immediately drew my attention. It read: **FOR YOUR EYES ONLY. PRIVATE AND CONFIDENTIAL.**

CHAPTER

29

AFTER READING THE LAST PAGE of the fax, Sophie and I sat for a long moment in Augie's quiet study not saying a word.

"Well, that was quite a surprise," I weakly offered.

"I'll say," was her response.

We lapsed into silence once again. In the last half hour or so, I had experienced a variety of contradictory emotions. First came the pleasure I felt when I saw that Madge had been successful in locating in the vast Yale archives what looked like the complete typewritten script and sheet music plus other ancillary material for the first original musical revue I had produced and directed there. I felt a bit of trepidation as we read through it. Would this all-student production be as good as my classmates and some critics had said it was? Well, I had mixed feelings on that score. It was clearly the work of the very young. It was brash, energetic, cheeky if not exceedingly risqué. It pulled very few punches. It delighted in puncturing many of Ivy League academia's most treasured hot air-filled traditions in general and in butchering many of Yale's most sacred cows in particular. As I said, it was clearly the work of the very young.

Its title appropriately enough was "Stuffed Quail," and it was not coincidental that the name of this type of poultry rhymed with that of our beloved *alma mater*. It was made abundantly clear throughout the revue's two outrageous acts that our "nourishing mother" (the literal translation of *alma mater* from the Latin) was herself overnourished, overstuffed with pretensions and was in for the feather plucking of her almost three-hundred year existence. Or so we had hoped.

Some of the lethal barbs were truly funny, successful and merited. Certain stuffed shirted professors; certain archaic conventions, customs, institutions and morés; certain accepted if minor prejudices and highfalutin attitudes deserved to be skewered and dragged screaming and kicking into the glaring light of ridicule.

Other attacks unfortunately, I now saw in hindsight, were not funny at all. When we deviated from making fun of the high and mighty who could take care of themselves and aimed our ridicule at those less fortunate, those less able to fight back, then we were in deep trouble. Then we were merely cruel. Then we were acting merely as privileged, insensitive bullies. The emotion I felt when I read the lines or lyrics that targeted those less fortunate, too easy victims was shame: unmitigated, unadulterated shame.

I felt this now the strongest in the song number that concluded the first act. This was the number that had apparently informed the "Macbeth" themed nightmare I had yesterday. It was the title song of the show and it was a disgrace. And as we discovered by reading the remainder of the fax, it had caused a great deal of trouble for several people.

As I had remembered at the theme bistro, the song that we parodied was "Nice 'N' Easy" a standard that Frank Sinatra had made popular. The point of the original song was that a mature love relationship should not be hurried, but rather each step in the process should be slowly and gradually enjoyed, treasured and emotionally watered till the relationship blossoms into a fully nourished love bouquet. How's that for an overripe metaphor?

Of course in our revue, we turned the song on its head. It now became a recipe for lust not love, a how-to lesson on scoring without the need for falling in love at all. And the available "quail," a term then frequently used to refer to young available women who were such easy prey to our own Yale bucks, were the local girls who lived in and around the town of New Haven. Many of these local blue collar "townies" did indeed have a reputation for being fast and "easy" targets for the often wealthy and more worldly university students.

The scene that I had staged in the revue featured two young Yale studs (named, what else, Biff and Cliff) introducing a younger, more innocent fraternity brother (the ingenuous Buffy) to the easy pickings available among the quail of New Haven. Pretty offensive, politically incorrect and sexist stuff I guess, but the worst and ultimately most harmful part of it came at the end of the final chorus. By the way, I noticed that the three words from this song that had reappeared in my dream (*road, problem* and *crime*) were lyrics from the original that remained intact in the parody. Photos from the production which were also included in Madge's fax showed the two older students dressed like Sinatra in his bobby socks heartthrob days. Buffy was dressed in stereotypical preppie garb and wore a Yale freshman beanie.

BIFF:	New Haven quails are easy
CLIFF:	And Yalie males are sleazy.
BOTH:	Who needs to fall in love?
BIFF:	Hey, Buffy, save your money.
	No need to pay for honey.
BUFFY:	No need to fall in love?
CLIFF:	Hey, buddy, save your moolah.

	Don't pay for boola boola.
BUFFY:	No need to fall in love!
BIFF:	You're on the road to scoring.
CLIFF:	You're sure to play.
BOTH:	So no need for any quail to wing away.
BUFFY:	The problem now of course is
	To play or pass my courses.
	To flunk would be a crime.
ALL:	Still 'Haven quails are worth it
	every time.

The concluding photo of this scene showed that another male actor had now entered dressed in drag like a trashy, New Haven teenage "townie" in mini-skirt, halter top and penny loafers. "She" carried a placard in front of her face that contained a large blown up photograph of the face of an actual local New Haven "favorite" whom I now recalled. Her character's name was Easy Weezy.

EASY WEEZY:	Yes, Easy Weezy does it every time.
BIFF:	Sure, Easy Weezy does it,
CLIFF:	Right, Easy Weezy does it,
ALL FOUR:	Yeah, Easy Weezy does it every time.

Curtain. Followed by tumultuous applause I was sure.

I now vaguely remembered that after a minimal discussion I had agreed with the writer of the song parody to allow the large photograph of the face of the notorious local 'townie' to appear on stage. What a moment of theatrical verité, I'm sure I thought. What an ultimate and hilarious shocker for the audience, I'm sure I believed. What a great first act curtain! And whom would it hurt anyway? The girl in question probably would never come to the show, and, even if she did or heard about it afterwards, she'd probably consider it a real hoot, a great opportunity to parade in her own fifteen minutes of fame. So whom would it hurt anyway?

I was pretty sure I now remembered who had written that scene and the lyrics to the parody. Checking the included faxed program and the song's sheet music confirmed my suspicions. The scene and new lyrics had been penned by Charlie Wetherstone.

Following the script, sheet music and production photos there was a handwritten personal note to Sophie from Madge Magill.

Sophie,
In addition to the script and photos of the show that you requested, I've taken it upon myself to include a corollary file. It was cross referenced to the file for "Stuffed Quail." It refers to disciplinary action which was taken as a result of the revue. The matter apparently was very hush hush at the time, and this file was marked Confidential. However, since over twenty five years have elapsed since the disciplinary action was taken and, even more importantly, since you text messaged me that these documents may provide some help in a murder investigation, I've elected to send you this additional file.

I've marked this fax as "Private and Confidential" and "For Your Eyes Only." I know you will be careful that this information is not disseminated.

It was good to hear from you. Let's get together the next time you're in New Haven.
All the best,
Madge
P.S. Apparently someone else was interested in seeing the file on "Stuffed Quail". The records indicate that three years ago my then assistant made a copy of the show's file and sent it to someone. I can't read the name or address of the party who requested it. My assistant at the time has since married and moved to

the west coast. I could try to contact her to see if she can decipher her handwriting and provide me with the name of the person who made the request, if you think that would be of any help. Probably coincidental, though.

M

Following Madge's note was a portion of Charlie's student file. Apparently the girl called "Easy Weezy" whose photograph was shown on stage had seen the show after all or at least had heard about it. Or perhaps her family had. In any event, primarily because the girl was underage, a top secret inquiry had been made by the University on the girl's behalf. Charlie's record had not been sterling for most of that year anyway. There had already been many disciplinary reports concerning his drinking and marijuana use. Added to this, his authoring the scene identifying the young girl in question by her own nickname and photograph were too much for the disciplinary committee. To protect the girl's reputation, her name was never listed in the file, and no mention of the inquiry was ever published. However, Charlie was expelled two weeks after the revue was presented.

I had heard rumors that Charlie had been involved in some monkey business involving young girls but had never learned the details. He had never broached the subject to Sophie or me either.

"Whew!" Sophie had breathed. I never heard anything about these repercussions, did you?"

"Not really, no."

"If we could find out who that girl is, it wouldn't be difficult to find someone who had it in for poor Charlie, that's for sure."

"Don't you know, Sophie?" I asked quizzically.

"No, do you?"

"Look closely at the photo of the girl's face in the picture."

"There is something familiar about her, but it's not in such great focus and after all it was taken twenty-five years ago."

"Her nickname was 'Easy Weezy.'"

"Right. So?"

"Do you remember the old television sitcom *The Jeffersons?*" I asked. "George Jefferson's pet name for his wife was 'Weezy.'"

"Yeah, I seem to remember that. And it was short for.... Oh, my God," Sophie cried.

"That's right, Sophie, it was a nickname for 'Louise.' Look at that picture again. 'Easy Weezy' is Louise Freemount."

CHAPTER
30

"ALL THIS TIME I WAS sure that Louise looked familiar to me," I said excitedly. "Even though it has been over twenty-five years since I've seen her and I never really knew her very well then, there was still something about her I recognized. She was always known as 'Easy Weezy' then. She was one of several young, pretty and incredibly loose girls from the town who hung around with university students. The ones I had run into had been veritable groupies of a few of the wild young men at the Drama School. And Charlie I'm afraid was one of the wildest. In fact, I believe I remember that he had brought her into the joint where I worked part time as night bartender once or twice. Although she couldn't have been more than fifteen, she was heavily made up, with big hair and the skimpiest of outfits. I'm sure that the last time he brought her into the bar, her forged I.D. was spotted and the proprietor called the police. Instead of being frightened, she had refused to provide the cops with her real name and address and only would identify herself as 'Easy Weezy' much to Charlie's delight and the policemen's chagrin. I don't remember the outcome other than they both were hauled off to the hoosegow amid peals of laughter."

"It must have been hysterical," Sophie replied with a grim expression.

"What must her parents have been like to allow a young girl like that to behave in that manner? And she was only fifteen?"

"She was certainly not any older than that."

"It seems unbelievable that 'Easy Weezy' grew up to be the 'hostess with the mostess' Louise Freemount. Have you any idea how that happened, Harry? I wonder what her whole story is. She told us that she was brought up by her grandparents in the Midwest, didn't she?"

"That's right, Sophie. Boy, do you have a good memory. And she was heartbroken when they died."

"And she never let on that she even knew Charlie. Do you remember how she said she felt sorry for *us* because of Charlie's apparent relapse?"

As Sophie reminded me of the dinner conversation around the Freemount table Sunday night, I remembered Louise and Augie's reaction to my spirited defense of Charlie, and the strange look they gave each other. I remembered that Louise's eyes had then filled up with tears and she had empathetically patted my hand. I also then thought back to Louise's response at Charlie's funeral when I had thanked her for attending and for seeing to it that the others had come as well: "No one should go through a loss like this alone," she had said quietly wiping away her tears.

"So what does all this mean, Sophie? Why did she never acknowledge knowing Charlie or me at Yale? Could Louise have been harboring thoughts of revenge all these years for Charlie's treatment of her in that revue? Could Louise have had anything to do with the terrible snow globes that were sent to him the past three years? Could Louise and perhaps Augie have had anything to do with Charlie's death? Should we be concentrating our attention on the Freemounts rather than Randy? Or are all three of them somehow mixed up in all this? Maybe Belinda meant evil *triplets* rather than twins? Oh, it's all too preposterous to even consider."

"Preposterous or not, something terrible's been going on around here, that's for sure. And we have the bodies of Charlie Wetherstone and Robert Gregory to prove it." Sophie then looked me straight in the eyes as she continued. "And there's one way we can start unraveling the preposterous from the factual. And that's for you, my dear Harry, to march yourself right over, right now, to Louise Freemount's Pilates studio and ask, no demand, that she start telling you the truth. We now know that she had a relationship with Charlie, an ultimately unpleasant one, when she was a kid, and we owe it to Charlie to find out what really happened. I wouldn't doubt that all the weeping and soup spilling and what not that Louise has exhibited the past few days are signs that she wants to come clean with the past. And you're just the fellow to convince her to do just that."

Before I could respond to Sophie's oration, I was startled by the sound of the fax machine behind us printing another page. It was another note to Sophie from Madge Magill.

> Sophie,
> Just looked once again at my assistant's note. This time through a magnifying glass. Though I still can't make out for sure the name of the person who requested the file on "Stuffed Quail" three years ago, the address looks like a post office box number (P.O. Box 334 or maybe 339) in the town of Hastings Corner. Since I'm sure that's the next town over from where you are now, Brookfield, I thought it might be of some interest to you. Hope it helps,
> Madge
> P.S. I've gotten rather excited about being involved in a murder investigation, even tangentially. You will let me know what you find out, won't you?
> M

At the bottom of this fax was a copy of the assistant's note. The address looked more like *P.O. Box 339, Hastings Corner* to me, but

Sophie thought it looked more like 334 to her. The box owner's name was indeed quite difficult for both of us to read. However, whether it was wishful thinking or not, the party's last name certainly looked to both of us like it began with an *F* and ended with what could easily have been an *NT*.

"That settles it," said Sophie. "You now absolutely have to see Louise and get to the bottom of all this. Did she secretly request a copy of the revue's file to be sent to her in care of a post office box in a nearby town? Did she need it as proof that it was Charlie who publicly humiliated her? Did she then start sending him those snow globes? I can't wait a minute longer to find out the truth. Please, Harry, you have to go see her right away. You knew her when she was a girl, and you can use that acquaintance to get her to own up to the truth, I know you can. Show her these faxes and she'll spill the beans as she did the onion soup, I know she will. Here are your car keys and your cell phone. Here's Louise's card with her studio's address. Call me the minute you've finished talking to her. Good luck! You can do it. Bye!"

I was out the door, inside the car and halfway down the driveway before I knew what I was doing. Then giving it a bit of thought I realized Sophie had been right. It was time I got the truth from Louise, whatever it might be. I punched in the address of her exercise studio and let Mandy lead me there. I also located in the GPS memory bank the address of the post office in nearby Hastings Corner and programmed it as a possible destination just in case a visit there might prove necessary, even though it was three years ago that it was used to receive the copied file from Yale.

After driving for a few minutes, my thoughts cascaded from Louise and Augie to Randy and from Randy to the callbacks scheduled this evening. The fax messages from Madge had distracted Sophie and me from preparing the necessary sides. I took out my cell phone to call Sophie about this and noticed it was not turned on. I did so and was surprised when it instantly rang to inform me there was one missed call waiting for me. I went into voice mail and listened to the message with interest. It was from Frank Gerrardi

"Hey Harry! I've just completed my first stop and it was a real doozie. I flew into a small airport near Cleveland and then took a cab to the first address that was in Charlie's van. It was a large factory which manufactured all sorts of collectibles and miniatures for wholesale distribution. When I entered the factory I said that I was a friend of Charles Wetherstone who had been there recently. I was introduced to the president of the company, Sam Blackthorn, an elderly gent who resembled the jovial Mr. Fezziwig of Dickens' "A Christmas Carol." His disposition was as sweet and charitable as his Victorian look-alike, and he told me how much he had enjoyed meeting Charlie and showing him around the factory, especially when he had learned that Charlie had received five snow globes that had been custom made for him there. He was shocked and deeply saddened when I told him of Charlie's death. When I asked him to tell me all that he had told Charlie, he was more than willing to oblige. He showed me the five clay models for the snow globes that Charlie had received. Since the sixth one had just been mailed to Brookfield, he told me that he had not shown the model to Charlie so as not to ruin the surprise. But he showed it to me. It was pretty spooky seeing the original clay figure of Lucy Ricardo holding the vitamin tonic bottle and spoon. He had shown Charlie the original drawings and photographs that had been sent to his factory by the person who had commissioned each of the snow globes. Each design had been accompanied by a fully operational sound chip when it was submitted to the factory six months before the globes were to be completed and mailed to Charlie at whatever address the gift giver had provided. "I guess Mr. Wetherstone had been a big movie and television buff," he laughingly said to me. When I asked Mr. Blackthorn for the name of the person who had commissioned and designed the globes, he was at first reluctant to tell me, as it had been agreed that the gift giver's identity would *always remain a secret. But I told him that I would very much like to contact this person to tell him how much Charlie had enjoyed the presents and to break the sad news of Charlie's death to him in person. This lie convinced Mr. Blackthorn that he was now no longer obligated to keep the person's identity a secret, and he laughed when he told me that it was not a "he" at all but a "she" who had commissioned and paid the rather hefty sums to custom design the snow globes. He had had several pleasant phone conversations with her over the years as well and had enjoyed working with her on the globes. He then showed me the address of "Mr. Wetherstone's lovely and generous benefactress" as Mr. Blackthorn called her. Hold on to your hat, Harry. The orders for the snow globes had come from a Miss Weezy Freemount c/o P.O. Box 334, Hastings Corner. Mr. Blackthorn had once asked her the derivation of her unusual first name. She had told him it was short for Louise. Can you beat that, Harry? Mr. Blackthorn also gave me the address of the company that had manufactured the sound chips. It's one of the addresses Charlie had that I had intended to visit today. I guess I can skip that now. And get this! He also told me that he had worked with Weezy on another totally different series of snow globes, and he gave me the name and address of the person to whom they had been sent. The person is named G. Bogart. I'm going to go there next. It's not far from the factory. I'll let you know what I find there. Can you believe it about Louise Freemount? I'll speak to you soon. Take care, Harry. Give my best to Hazel and Sophie."*

I shut the phone off and drove the remaining few blocks to the Pilates studio in a state of shock and amazement. So it was indeed Louise who was behind all this? Could this all be true? I certainly now had plenty with which to confront her. And somehow I now was welcoming this confrontation. The sense of anger I had felt a number of times since finding Charlie's body flooded over me once again. I parked the car in front of the attractive studio, not really noticing the women who were leaving the building chattering about this and that apparently having just completed one of Louise's Pilates classes. Holding the faxed pages tightly in my hand, I opened the front door and walked in.

The front room was empty, but the door to the large inner room was open. I peered inside and to my astonishment saw that Augie and Louise were both at the far end of the empty room calmly sitting on two folding chairs.

"Hello, Harry," Augie said quietly to me. "We've been waiting for you."

CHAPTER

31

speechless: adjective   **1.** Lacking the faculty of speech or temporarily unable to speak, as through astonishment.   **2.** Refraining from speech; silent.   **3.** Unexpressed or inexpressible in words: *speechless admiration*

YES, YES INDEED TO DEFINITION 1. A moment or two later I was able to speak, but I didn't. See definition 2. Definition 3?   I'm afraid Webster got it right there as well. I did in some strange twisted way admire both Augie and Louise at that moment for the calm almost serene state in which they appeared to be sitting there so still, so patiently waiting for me to make my first, dramatic response to Augie's "We've been waiting for you."

And so with a deep breath I did: "Oh yeah?"

I'm afraid this was not one of my most memorable interjections. But it served its purpose by getting the ball rolling. Augie said, "Yes, Harry. You see, you didn't have to bring your copy of the fax here. We have our own." And he looked from the faxed pages I was hugging to my chest down to those neatly stacked on the floor next to him. As he noticed my incredulous look, he explained, "My fax machine is networked to printers both in my study at home and in my office at the hospital. So when you received one copy of the fax from Yale, I simultaneously received another.

After reading it, I drove here to discuss the situation with Louise. We realized it was now time to talk openly with you. So we called your cell phone. When we reached your voice mail, we tried Sophie's phone. When I told her we read the fax and wanted to talk to you, she advised us that you were on your way here. So, we've been waiting for you."

"All right, now I'm here. So let us indeed talk." I had regained both the faculty of speech and my anger. "What is all this about? Louise, why did you keep our acquaintance at Yale a secret? Why did you never mention that you knew Charlie whom you certainly knew a lot better than you..."

"Yes, a lot better than I knew you, a lot better, "Louise interrupted with a sad smile. "I'm sorry we've had to hold so much back from you, Harry. We never wanted to, but, you see, we felt we had no choice."

"No choice!" I exploded. For heaven's sake, Louise, Charlie's dead!"

"We're well aware of that, Harry," Augie then quickly added," but I would very much appreciate it if we could discuss this in a civil, rational manner. There's no need to use that tone to my wife."

"Oh, there isn't? Well, I'm afraid I shall have to use whatever tone..."

"Please," the quiet sincerity in Louise's voice stopped the tirade that was about to erupt from within me. "Augie, thank you for trying to protect me once again, but please let me try to handle this myself, and, Harry, please give me a chance to explain. Please sit next to us. Please."

There was such pain in Louise's voice that I had no choice but to pull over a folding chair and, still a bit begrudgingly, sit down a few feet in front of them.

"Thank you, Harry." She then paused for a moment or two, apparently dredging up from within herself the strength to continue. She took a long, deep breath and began.

"As you must now have remembered, when I was a young teenager growing up in New Haven, I was derisively known to just about everyone in town and to many at the University by the very apt nickname of Easy Weezy. And *easy* was what I was, and reckless, and self-destructive, and self-loathing, and self-pitying and angry. Oh yes, very, very angry.

"Angry at being born into a family that was not rich or even middle-class. Angry at being born into a family that was not sophisticated or witty or beautiful like the movie stars I read about in the fan magazines I stole from the corner store and fantasized about at night. Angry at being born into a family of seven kids all born within a very few years of each other and all fighting a losing battle for a break in a culture that didn't notice them. Born to blue collar parents who were full time religious zealots more concerned with the rewards of the afterlife than with providing love or support or a sense of self worth to their offspring. Parents who were especially distrustful and severe to their youngest and only daughter.

"Constantly lectured about the evils of the flesh and moral dissipation, I did of course the very opposite of what they preached and flocked to them, selecting friends who smoked and drank and did drugs. Sneaking out at night from the time I was twelve, I ran wild with my girl friends and always was attracted to the boys at the University, who seemed to have everything I did not and craved: sophistication, money, natural and unassailable shortcuts to the world of riches and fame and intellect and success. And in a desperate effort to get my foot into this totally bewitching and unknown world, I allowed the Yalies access to much more than my foot.

"And then when I was not quite fifteen, I met Charlie, and for the first time in my life I fell in love. Sure, he was a graduate student and I was still a kid of fourteen. Sure, he ran with a wild group of other seemingly glamorous theater students and had lots of other girls, but he was bright and artistic and funny and basically kind to me and often gentle. And I loved him, and he was the only boy I gave myself to completely. The night we were taken to the local jail because I had a fake I.D. and I refused to identify myself, a police doctor cursorily gave me a routine physical and then asked me if I were pregnant. I laughed my head off over that ridiculous scenario as I laughed about just about everything: my life, my lack of education, my future, my lack of prospects. Imagine me, bad little Easy Weezy, a mother. Ridiculous! Charlie also got a good laugh about this impossible occurrence when I gigglingly told him what the idiotic doctor had suggested. And then, lo and behold, I found out it was true.

"But when my caring and loving parents caught me upchucking behind the garage one morning, and forced me to confess the truth and identify Charlie as the father, they went on a rampage. The discovery of my condition came just at the time that my father had seen that publicity shot from 'Stuffed Quail' outing me to the entire world as Easy Weezy in the local paper. My good Christian parents wanted only revenge. They went to the school and had Charlie expelled. They not only wanted him out of the way but they wanted me and my embarrassing condition taken care of as well. Of course, abortion was not a possibility for them, so they sent me to my grandmother in Ohio and there, pretty much, I stayed for the next ten years or so. Thank heavens.

"Everything my parents weren't, my mother's father and mother were. They lived in a small farming community from which my mother ran away after she had met the traveling evangelist who became my father and moved to Connecticut with him.   My mother had had very little to do with my grandparents after that.   And so, my grandparents had been happy to take me in and raise me pretty much as their own. They never judged me or my wild ways. Rather, they tried to understand me and helped me to begin to rethink my life and how I had cavalierly and laughingly been throwing it away. And they did it not with sanctimonious fire and brimstone sermons and savage denunciations as my folks had done, but with kindness and true concern. Unfortunately, the baby was born dead. I held his little inert body in my arms only once. If he had lived, I think I might eventually have learned to be a good mother to him."

"And Charlie never knew anything about the pregnancy?"

"No. I never had the chance to tell him. He left town immediately after he was expelled. But I don't think I would have told him even if I had seen him again. The way he had guffawed at the ridiculous idea that I could ever be a mother probably would have prevented me. And later I finally realized that he had never loved me. I had been a fun and exciting playmate for him. Nothing more. Just the fact that he had used me as a device to get a big laugh in the school show proved that."

"I'm really ashamed about my part in that escapade, Louise."

"Don't worry about it now, Harry. My parents' reaction to the picture from that show and my pregnancy turned out to be the best things that could have happened to me. They got me away from a life that was never going to go anywhere but down."

And as Louise continued talking about how her life and attitude had improved while living with her grandparents, something was nagging at me. It was that feeling of *déjà vu* that I had experienced the second time I had been in the coffee shop. I knew I had experienced this scene before or something very much like it. I looked at the three of us sitting on folding chairs while Louise recounted the story of her life, and suddenly it hit me. This moment was an incredible parallel to my experience in the hanger at dawn Monday morning. Sophie, Frank, Hazel and I had been seated on similar folding chairs listening to Hazel tell us about her life before and after meeting Charlie. It was uncanny that now in the Pilates studio a woman was telling me once again about her life before and after meeting Charlie. In both histories, the woman's relationship with Charlie ultimately caused her to improve her life. Only this time, Louise's life improved only after Charlie was no longer in the picture.

As Louise continued on about how her knowledge and interest in both cooking and Pilates had both derived from her grandmother's skills in these areas, I let myself think more about other unlikely parallels I had encountered since arriving in Brookfield. Not only had it been I who found both dead men's bodies, but the way Robert Gregory had died mirrored exactly the way Belinda's husband had met his death. Charlie was the second set designer who had died in Brookfield recently. The previous Barn Theater technical director and set designer had died only last month in a car accident. His death had provided an opening for Charlie to fill. Robert Gregory had not been the only diabetic I had met in Brookfield. There had also been the bizarre meeting with Rhoda the diabetic cat at the place where Robert had died. Randy rode a motorcycle and apparently it was he who had given Frank and me a devilish chase when he stole the snow globe and Charlie's laptop. Belinda had hysterically mentioned a motorcycle in her ravings at *The Green Parrot*. That was where she had mentioned twins, evil twins. There certainly had been a number of twinned occurrences and coincidences among the evil we had encountered during the past four days in Brookfield.

Louise was now mentioning how her life had taken a blessed turn after she met Augie because of the mix-up at the hotel in Chicago. My mind instantly darted back to the Brookfield Inn this morning where Lucy had so viciously snarled in the reception area. Suddenly my consciousness stopped streaming in this macabre direction as I heard Louise begin to recount the strange happenings that began three years ago.

"So Augie and I had been happily married for four years when I received the first package."

My ears pricked up. "Package, did you say?"

"Yes. It arrived by UPS a week after we had returned from my grandmother's funeral, so I was still rather upset and this was why I reacted so strongly to it."

"It didn't contain a snow globe by any chance?" I asked with a catch in my throat.

"Snow globe? No it didn't. But it's funny you should say that. It actually contained something else associated with children." Louise's eyes began to tear as she continued softly, "It contained a baby doll."

"A doll?" I repeated.

"Yes," Augie now spoke since it seemed difficult for Louise to go on. "And when you squeezed the damned thing, it said two words: Mamma Weezy."

Chapter

32

"And I suppose you received a similar package twice a year."

The three of us jumped when we heard the voice and quickly turned around to see Sophie standing in the open doorway behind us. "I'm sorry to have startled you. I got here as soon as I could, Harry. Please, Louise, answer my question. Was the doll the only package you received?"

It was Augie who replied. "No, Sophie, as you somehow already seem to know, the doll was only the first unpleasant surprise delivered to Louise. And, you are right, she received two of them a year for the past three years. They arrived each year on the same dates."

"Let me take a wild guess, Augie," Sophie interrupted. "Did Louise receive them on the eleventh of May and then again on the eleventh of August?"

Both of the Freemounts now stared at Sophie in astonishment. "How did you know that?" Louise gasped.

"I'll let you know in a minute. But first tell us what else you received." Sophie then pulled up a chair and sat next to me. She patted my hand as we waited for Augie's reply.

"That infernal talking doll was delivered on May 11th. There was no return address, nor any note of explanation of any kind. Then three months later, another UPS package arrived. This one contained only a baby's rattle. The next May there arrived a baby's bottle followed by a teething ring in August. Last year came a miniature teddy bear and a pair of bronzed baby shoes. Then just the other evening, the pattern suddenly changed. Instead of a *package* mailed to her, Louise came across an envelope, a blank sealed envelope that somehow had been brought into the kitchen. Without thinking, she opened it and found..."

"A card on which cutout letters from magazines had been pasted," I said.

"Yes, that's right, Harry," Augie said with an ironic look. "Although I ripped it up as soon as I saw it and threw it in the trash, I noticed that you had found at least a piece of it when I saw you and Sophie later that night."

"Actually, I was the one who had done the snooping in the trash," Sophie volunteered. "Did we guess correctly that it was a birthday message to you, Louise?"

"Yes, a malicious one," Louise said her voice beginning to quiver. "The card read: 'Happy Birthday Louise.'"

"But you told us your birthday is not in May," I said.

"That's right, Harry," she replied, a slow tear running down her cheek. But my baby was born on May 11th all those many years ago. The card meant that this was the day I gave birth. It was the day I held him for the one and only time moments after he had passed. So, on this May 11th, when I opened the envelope and read this sickest of all possible sick jokes, I screamed and toppled the pot of soup on the stove and..."

Augie held her tightly in his arms, and all was silent in the studio except for Louise's muffled sobs. Inside my skull, however, my mind was racing at the speed of light. So May 11th was when Louise's baby had been born. But why had both Charlie and Louise received half of their semi-annual gifts on August 11? Why a date exactly three months after the first? What significance was there to three months? Three months. Wait a minute, an incandescent bulb suddenly switched on in my brain. If viewed the other way around, there was a period of nine months between August and May. Nine months! Were the gifts to Charlie and Louise, the father and mother of the tragic infant, sent to them as vicious reminders of the dates of his conception and birth?

I couldn't wait to discuss this possibility with Sophie, but right now she was posing another question since Louise had composed herself a bit. "Were you aware of these packages from the beginning, Augie?" she asked.

"Yes, in fact I happened to be with Louise when she opened the first one. Her reaction to the doll was so extreme that she had no choice but to tell me the story of her life in New Haven and its consequences."

"I had been so afraid that if I told Augie all the details of my past, I would lose him. But I should have known better. He has been so kind and supportive that I honestly think all this has brought us even closer together."

"Did you go to the police to see if they could discover who sent you these things and prosecute that person?" I asked.

"Augie wanted to, but I asked him not to," Louise said softly. "You see, I've always been pretty sure who it was."

"You have?" Sophie and I responded in unison.

"Yes, and that's why I didn't identify myself to you, Harry, when we met again after all these years and it was clear that you weren't able to recognize me. I didn't want to hurt you, so I never said a word."

"What do you mean, Louise?"

"I'm sorry, Harry and Sophie, but I have always been sure that it was Charlie who sent those packages to me."

"Charlie!" once again Sophie and I bellowed our disbelief with one voice.

"Of course. Who else could it have been? Each of the few people who knew I had been pregnant and lost the baby had died by the time I received the doll. My grandmother was the last and she died a week before the first package arrived. Only Charlie was left."

"I don't understand, Louise," Sophie said. "You just said that you never told Charlie that you were pregnant."

"That's true, but I didn't tell you that ten years ago Charlie called my mother. She told me about this phone call a few months later. I had come back to New Haven to see her as she was seriously ill. In fact she died several days after we had our talk. In a way we were able to resolve many of our differences at that time, so it was a blessing that I made the trip. Anyway, she told me then that Charlie had phoned because he wanted to reach me. Because her vendetta against him had caused Charlie to be expelled, she was embarrassed to talk to him. She told him that I no longer lived in the east and wasn't sure where I was living now. To get rid of him, my mother gave him my grandmother's address in Ohio."

"Had Charlie told your mother why he wanted to reach you?" I asked.

"He never told her, but she assumed he had found out somehow after all these years that it was because of me that he had been expelled and wanted to get back at me in some way. I can only assume that he traced me through my grandmother's address and then found out about the baby. It must have been because of his alcoholism that he chose to have his revenge on me in this sad way."

"In this very sick way is how I would put it," Augie said. "If Louise hadn't insisted that I do nothing, I would have put a stop to this."

"And then when we heard that both you and Charlie would be spending the summer here at Brookfield, it seemed like a miracle. I thought that I could finally be able to have a long talk with Charlie that would result in some sort of reconciliation between us, as I had had with my mother before she died. But, tragically, his demons prevented that." Louise's eyes were filling up again.

"Louise, Augie, listen to me," I said. "I know for a fact that it was not Charlie who was doing this, sending you these packages."

"Oh, come now, Harry, how can you say that?"

"I can say it, Augie, because Charlie was also receiving packages in the mail intended to wound him psychologically. And he also received them twice a year for the last three years on the eleventh of May and the eleventh of August."

"Oh, please, that can't be true. If he told you that, he must have been lying and trying to cover up his own actions."

"No, Augie, it's true," Sophie said. The last package was delivered to his bungalow after he had died. It was sent back to the UPS office in town. It was a custom designed snow globe intended to be as damaging to him as the baby items were to Louise. We have it, and his fiancée and Frank Gerrardi both corroborated the existence of the other five."

"And," I continued, "we have been doing some investigations on our own as to who ordered the construction of these snow globes. Frank flew to Cleveland today, and he found out some very disturbing information. I'm sorry to have to ask you this, Louise, but do you have a post office box in Hastings Corner?"

"Do I what?" she asked with surprise. "No, of course not. What are you talking about?"

I took out my cell phone. "Frank left a message for me a little while ago. I want you to hear what he found. Sophie, you haven't heard this yet."

I then played on speaker phone Frank's message about his meeting with the president of the factory. I carefully watched the faces of Louise and Augie. They seemed genuinely astonished by what they heard."

After the message ended, Louise said, "But this is insane. I don't know anything about this post office box nor about these snow globes, whatever they are. This is some sort of crazy mistake."

"Or some one is certainly trying his best to frame Louise. It's patently ridiculous." Augie was becoming very angry. "And I'm going to find out who's been doing this to poor Louise, and God help him."

"Did you read Madge Magill's second fax to me, Augie?" Sophie asked.

"There was a second one? No I came over to see Louise immediately after reading the one I have here."

Taking the second fax from me and handing it to the Freemounts, Sophie said, "Someone also using the same post office box requested the file on the revue from Yale three years ago. Although the name is difficult to read, it looks a lot like *Freemount* to me."

They looked at the receipt incredulously. "None of this is true, Harry, I swear it. I know nothing about this post office box. Nothing." Louise's face had turned ashen.

"Of course you don't, darling," said Augie. "And we'll prove it. I say we all drive over to Hastings Corner right now and settle this matter once and for all."

And so we did.

CHAPTER

33

IN A PLAY I HAD directed once, a character who was an ex-sailor used the navy slang term "Pucker Factor" to refer to a tense situation caused by high stress. The phrase was derived from the fact that one's sphincter tends to tighten up or 'pucker' involuntarily during such times. So, it was undeniably accurate to say that the pucker factor was extremely high during our forty-minute silent car ride to Hastings Corner, a community which turned out to be much more rural than Brookfield.

The silence was finally broken by Mandy's confident announcement that we had reached our destination. For the first time, however, I was forced to question Mandy's accuracy. Although we had reached the address given for the Hastings Corner Post Office, we found ourselves parked outside a rather ramshackle old building whose overhead sign proclaimed in large lettering: *General Store, Silverheels Seagull Proprietor.*

"I thought this was supposed to be the post office," I said.

"We wouldn't know," Augie replied. "Neither Louise nor I has ever been here."

"Wait a minute, look at that little sign to the right of the big one, next to the flag," Sophie pointed.

We did so and read in much smaller lettering: *U.S. Post Office, Silverheels Seagull Postmaster.*

The four of us climbed the three stairs, crossed the front porch lined with wooden rocking chairs and entered the front door. We were greeted by the sweet smell of incense and the soundtrack from "Easy Rider" quietly playing from overhead speakers. The place looked strangely like a much larger version of those head shops which had once proliferated in Greenwich Village and the Haight-Ashbury district of San Francisco. Posters promoting "Flower Power," "Hair: The Musical," and "Woodstock" lined the walls.

"Well, this certainly is a psychedelic time warp," Sophie laughed.

To prove her point, a voice from the corner of the room chimed in: "Hey baby, what's happening? *Que Pasa?*"

The elderly man sitting cross-legged on an Indian cushion strumming an acoustic guitar wore long beads around his neck, thick coke-bottle glasses and his silver hair long and straggly. And, I couldn't believe it, he then immediately went into a very decent impression of George Carlin's Al Sleet, the Hippy Dippy Weatherman.

"Today's weather forecast is brought to you by Parsons' Pest Control. Do you have termites, water bugs and roaches? Well, Parsons will help you get rid of the termites and water bugs and help you smoke the roaches! Hey! Today's weather is dominated by a large Canadian low which is not to be confused with a Mexican high! Hey! Tonight's forecast: Dark! Hey!"

I couldn't help applauding his routine enthusiastically. Sophie joined in, and although they didn't clap, it looked like the tension in the Freemounts' bodies had begun to decrease. Their pucker factors appeared substantially lower.

"Howdy, there, neighbors, what can I do you for?" he asked with a benevolent smile.

"Are we addressing, Mr., uh, Seagull," I asked.

"You are indeed, man, you are indeed. I take it from your little hesitation that you are a bit perplexed about my moniker. Is that right, man?"

"Well, it is rather unusual."

"Groovy, man, groovy. I changed my name legally as an *homage* to my two favorite celebrities. I took the name Seagull, when that great actress Barbara Hershey changed her last name to that in the '70s. When she was shooting a scene from that cool film "Last Summer," a seagull was tragically killed. My Barbara felt a sense of personal responsibility for that death and went by the name of Barbara Seagull professionally for a number of years thereafter as a tribute to the bird. She eventually changed her name back, but I never did. Did you know that Barbara and David Carradine produced a baby they named *Free*? Sadly, he has since changed his name to Tom."

"Well, that's very interesting, I'm sure, but we're here to…" Augie tried to interject.

But the postmaster continued his etymological dissertation unfazed by Augie's interruption. As he spoke, he punctuated the end of each sentence with a strum on his guitar. "My first name I changed in honor of my other great favorite. He also had been born with a different name, Harold Jay Smith. He was born on the Six Nations of the Grand River Indian Reserve in Ontario, Canada. But when he took the name of Jay Silverheels, his eternal fame was assured. Who could ever forget him as the Lone Ranger's devoted friend and companion, Tonto? Because he was instrumental in seeing to it that only Native Americans played themselves in the movies, I changed my first name so as always to remember that great man." With one final strum and the words, "Pretty cool, huh, man?" Silverheels Seagull was finally still long enough for Augie to speak.

"Please, we're here on a very serious mission."

"Well, then, *kemo sabe*, how can I help you?"

"It looks like someone has illegally used my wife's name in renting a post office box here. Box 334. Could you help us find out if that's the case?"

"That's a pretty heavy offense, man. What's your old lady's name?"

"My *wife's* name is Louise Freemount," Augie said clearly.

"Freemount, Freemount, that's a pretty groovy name, itself, man, and I remember that it struck my fancy when I first heard it. It reminded me of Barbara Seagull's son's name *Free* and another tube favorite of mine, Sergeant Preston of the Royal Canadian Mounted Police. And I remember she was a pretty groovy-looking chick when she rented the box. That was a number of years ago, wasn't it?"

"It was at least three years ago, we believe," I said.

"Yeah, that seems about right. Is your old la...uh, wife here now, man?" he asked Augie.

"Yes, I'm right here. I'm Louise Freemount. The real Louise Freemount." Louise's voice quavered a bit as she made this statement.

"Are you?" the hippy postmaster asked. Your voice sounds a bit different from what I remember. Could you step up closer to me? My eyes aren't what they once were. An unfortunate side effect for me and many other brother deadheads during the Age of Aquarius," he laughed.

Louise was now only inches away from his extremely thick glasses. "There's some resemblance there but no cigar. I think you're shorter than the chick who rented the box as well. And I seem to remember she used a different first name. Not Louise."

"Weezy?" Louise said softly.

"Yes, that's right. But one reason I can't remember her face too well was she always came round to pick up mail from her box while on her bike. The boxes can be reached from the outside on the side of the store."

"Bike?" I asked excitedly.

"Right. Weezy Freemount always drove her motorcycle to pick up her mail. So, I only saw her face the one time she filled out the request form. All the other times she was wearing her helmet."

"Well, that clinches it," Louise said. "I've never ridden a motorcycle in my life, even in the old days in New Haven."

At the first mention of a motorcycle, Sophie and I looked at each other, but neither of us said a word. It was too crazy an idea to consider seriously, wasn't it? There was no way Randy Williamson could have posed as a woman at the post office in Hastings Corner, was there?

I kept going over this ridiculous thought in my mind as Mr. Seagull granted Augie's request to look at the signature on the form completed to rent the box. Sophie helped them find it from the files. The annual rental fees had all been paid in cash. The name and address listed on the form were: *Weezy Freemount, Pemberley Cottage, Brookfield.* Louise pulled out her driver's license, and we compared the two signatures. It was clear that the signatures were very different. It seemed that Louise had not been the person who had rented the box and therefore had no connection with the snow globes or the request for the material on the revue produced at Yale.

'Although I've never been tight with the fuzz," Silverheels said, "if you want me to file a complaint about this matter, I'll be happy to do so, man."

"Not just yet, if you don't mind," I said quickly. "We would like to do a bit more investigating first. However, if the box holder should come round here for some reason, we'd appreciate your calling me. Here's my card."

"And here's mine," Augie said.

"Perhaps you could hold her under some pretext till we could get here?" Sophie suggested.

"Anything's possible, I suppose, man, for you know what they say," the postmaster responded with a laugh. And then sitting back down on his cushion, he began singing while accompanying himself on the guitar. As we walked out, we could still hear these words blowing in the wind:

> The line it is drawn
> The curse it is cast
> The slow one now
> Will later be fast
> As the present now
> Will later be past
> The order is
> Rapidly fadin'.
> And the first one now
> Will later be last
> For the times they are a-changin'.

"I hope he's right," Louise said with an enormous sigh.

"Of course, he's right, Louise," Sophie said hugging her. "We now know for sure that a third party sent those terrible packages both to you and Charlie. And we know this person falsely used your name to do so and drives a motorcycle. We're getting closer and closer. The times indeed are a-changin', and we'll find out who this creep is and see that justice has its day."

"Sophie's right, Louise. Please excuse us for doubting you, but we are all on the same side now, and we shall not stop until we identify that bastard," I said.

On the ride back to Brookfield, I added one more thing. "There has been a wild thought that's been bouncing around inside my skull since we left Hastings Corner. And I now have a plan in mind to determine if it is valid or not. Although Sophie doesn't know it yet, she and I are going to put this plan into action this very evening. And then who knows? Maybe, with good luck, we'll have an answer to this riddle by tomorrow."

I wouldn't tell the Freemounts anything further, but they seemed to be a bit more hopeful when we left them at the Pilates studio.

"So what's in your devious little mind, boss?" Sophie asked when the Freemounts had left us. "It has to do with Randy, right?"

"It does indeed, Sophie. And the callbacks tonight will be where we can begin to see if I'm on the right track or not."

"So we're off to the theater then?"

"After we make a slight detour. Follow me in your car, will you, my dear Watson."

Chapter

34

IT WAS NEARLY SIX O'CLOCK, and we had finally finished our preparations for the callback auditions. It had taken Sophie and me quite bit of time to work out the plan we were to follow this evening, but we were now satisfied with it and had printed and set out the newly required handouts. We had also tried out the equipment we had purchased prior to arriving at the theater, and all seemed to function properly.

It had also been necessary to call Frank Gerrardi to acquaint him with the role he was to play this evening. Miraculously to me, Frank had been instantly able to set up a conference call with Hazel's cell phone. She sounded much more relaxed, and we were relieved to hear that her drive today with Lucy had been pleasant. With my speakerphone on, Sophie could also hear and participate in our four-way phone conversation.

I first related to Frank and Hazel what we had discovered about Louise Freemount and her relationship with Charlie in New Haven. Frank then explained to Hazel what he had learned at the snow globe factory to which I then recounted why Sophie and I were now convinced that someone impersonating Louise had commissioned the globes.

Frank then told us his latest news. He reminded us that earlier today Sam Blackthorn, the genial factory owner, had told him that the party using the name of Weezy Freemount had also designed a second set of snow globes. Provided with the recipient's name and address, Frank had driven there from the factory. To his amazement, G. Bogart, the name he had been given, turned out to be Sister Gretchen Bogart, an elderly nun who was now living out her final days in contemplation at her order's nursing home.

"The novice who kindly led me to the small library where Sister Gretchen could be found told me that she was now quite frail and occasionally her mind might wander a bit. 'But she is a delightful person and one of our favorites here,' she told me.

When I entered the small but pleasant room, I saw the tiny old lady was dressed in full habit and was seated in a wheel chair next to an open window which looked out on a peaceful and sweet-smelling herb garden. She was peering at an object in her hand. When I got closer, I saw that it was a small snow globe. She was obviously enjoying slowly shaking it and watching the golden particles peacefully drifting down.

When I was introduced to her and we were left alone in the library, Sister Gretchen said to me with a sweet smile, 'Pardon me, young man, but you don't look familiar. You're not one of my children, are you?' When I asked her what she meant, she told me that for over forty years she had run the order's local orphanage. 'I may not remember all the names of the children who passed through our doors and our lives, but I'm still pretty good at recognizing their faces.' She then began to ramble on a bit about some of the children she particularly remembered who had stayed in touch with her over the years, visiting her and sending her pictures of their families and letting her know how successful their lives had turned out. I was thinking how to redirect the conversation to the snow globe, when she did so herself. 'And then there are those who keep in touch in different ways. They are the ones whose lives have sadly not been as happy or successful as the others. I think I love these children most of all.' She handed me the snow globe she had been holding. 'This was sent to me a few months ago with a typed note that read: From One of Your Kids. I have received snow globes like this one every few months, all with the same typed note. I've received them now for at least six or seven years. The others are over there on those shelves.'

I turned to where she had pointed and saw the score or so of glass globes shining in the light streaming in through the open window. The figures inside were all miniature Humphrey Bogarts depicting different scenes from his movies. I quickly recognized "The Maltese Falcon," "The Treasure of the Sierra Madre," and "The Big Sleep" among the many ingenious little glass bubbles. The one I was holding showed a tiny Bogart sitting at a small table with a miniature Ingrid Bergman. I asked her why Bogart and why snow globes.

She gave a tinkling little laugh. 'I'm afraid I've always been afflicted with the sin of pride. Since my last name is Bogart, I always told my children that I was a distant relative of the famous movie star, and I think I pretty much convinced myself that it was true. Plus I always loved snow globes. The ones that my parents had given me as a child were my most precious possessions, and I guess I communicated my love for them to my children over the years.' As I handed the latest globe back to her, she dreamily shook it and softly began quoting lines from the film as her eyes slowly closed. I remember hearing 'Of all the gin joints in all the towns in all the world, she walks into mine,' 'We'll always have Paris,' and 'Here's looking at you, kid' as she dozed off, and I quietly left."

"Wow, that is some story, Frank," Sophie murmured as she expressed what we all were feeling. "So an orphanage, huh? What does that mean? Louise told us her newborn baby boy had died."

"Yes, she did," I agreed. "But, for some strange reason, ever since I heard that in her shocked state Belinda had talked about *twins, evil twins* I have not been able to get the idea of twins out of my mind. What if Louise had given birth to twin boys and for some reason didn't know it or didn't remember it. Could that have been possible? And what if one twin survived and was sent without Louise's knowledge to Sister Gretchen's orphanage. Could that have been possible? And what if..."

"That surviving twin were Randy?" Hazel finished my thought.

"Exactly. He certainly is the right age. And what if Randy masqueraded as Weezy in his dealings on the phone with the owner of the factory and briefly in person three years ago with the hippie dippie postmaster with the thick glasses."

"It's a wild hypothesis, Harry," Frank responded.

"You can say that again, Frank. And if you want to hear wild, wait till I tell you about the idea Sophie and I have cooked up for tonight and what I'd like you to do. But first, would you be able to visit the orphanage that Sister Gretchen ran? And see if you can check their records for the date twenty-five years ago that Louise gave birth. See if any baby boys were brought in at that time."

"Will do, Harry. They must be closed now, but I'll stay over tonight and get there bright and early tomorrow morning."

I thanked Frank and then related to Hazel and him what our plan was for the callbacks. We had finalized all the details when we heard the first of the actors entering the lobby of the theater. With a meaningful look between us, Sophie left me in the auditorium while she returned to the lobby to greet the actors and give them the new handouts. I took a deep breath and crossed my fingers as I waited for Sophie to bring the sixteen actors in.

Two and a half hours later, at 8:30 pm, Sophie and I sat in the auditorium exhausted but satisfied as the last actor left the theater. I imagined I could hear Randy's motorcycle revving up and then taking off like a rocket from the parking lot.

The callbacks had gone exceedingly well. When Sophie had ushered the twelve men and four women into the auditorium, I greeted them warmly from the stage and asked them to take seats. I congratulated them for being chosen for this final round from the eighty-seven people who had auditioned for me over the weekend. I then told them I was seriously considering casting one of the two plays we would be performing this summer in a rather unorthodox manner. The play I had written called "The Readiness Is All" a serious modern political and psychological thriller utilizing many of the themes and situations found in Shakespeare's tragedies would be cast conventionally with four men and two women. However, I told them I was thinking of casting the second of my new plays, a raucous and physical farce thematically related to those of the Bard's comedies involving cross dressing and mistaken sexual identities, with an all male cast playing all the roles, male and female, as was common practice in the Elizabethan theater. I would only cast this second play which was titled "Or What You Will" in this way if I felt the male actors chosen could pull this feat off playing the three women's parts truthfully and convincingly without a trace of camp or exaggeration.

I then began the auditions by pairing off the women and men and asking them to read from the sides from the two plays previously given them. I took the liberty of mixing and matching the actors till I had a good idea in my mind who worked well with whom, which pairs exhibited the right amount of sexual chemistry, could play off each other the best, and so on. An hour later I had pretty well decided whom I would cast for the drama and whom I would cast for the comedy if I chose to cast it conventionally. I then thanked the women for their good work and told them all would be notified in a day or two advising them if they had been cast or not.

After the ladies had left, I then told the twelve men who remained that I would now have them read for the three female roles in the comedy. I reiterated to them that they should be as truthful as possible in finding and expressing their feminine side. I didn't want them to appear to an audience as female impersonators but rather be accepted quickly as authentic, realistic human beings who happened to be women. They were each to read from the new handouts Sophie had given them when they arrived this evening.

There were three monologues from my play each delivered by one of the three female characters: the first was a charming, confident, radiant leading lady; the second was an ingenue, younger than the first; the third was a character woman, a warm-hearted, street-wise working class servant.

I told them that they were now to work on these three monologues by themselves until they were comfortable enough with them and their interpretations to record them on one of the twelve mini-tape recorders I handed them. These were the ones Sophie and I had purchased on the way to the theater this afternoon. I told them I would then take the tapes back with me and review them for their truthfulness and accuracy in sounding believably like women as well as fully dimensional characters. In this way, I told them, I would not be influenced by seeing them dressed as they now were as men. I advised them to think of real women they knew who had some of these characters' qualities and try to represent these actual women as truthfully as they could.

While they each separated from the others and began to read the monologues and work on them quietly to themselves, Sophie and I alternately kept our eyes peeled on Randy, watching him carefully to see if he suspected anything. The main reason we had designed this exercise was for Randy to put his voice on tape attempting to sound as convincingly as possible as different types of women. We had asked Frank to ensure that Sam Blackthorn would be available at 9 o'clock to listen to Randy's tape and verify whether or not he recognized the voice as belonging to the Weezy Freemount with whom he had had several phone conversations. This afternoon I had also phoned Silverheels Seagull and asked if he would also make himself available to listen to the tape. Both men had kindly agreed to our requests.

One by one, each of the twelve actors recorded their tapes. After listening to their initial efforts, many chose to erase them and perform the monologues a second or even a third time. I had told them this would be perfectly permissable as I wanted them to be completely satisfied with their work and not feel pressured in any way by time constraints.

Finally, all had completed their tapes and handed their recorders to me and after thanking me for this opportunity left the theater. Maddeningly, Randy was the next to the last to finish and with a big smile said good night to us.

"I couldn't detect any sign that he found anything fishy about this recording business," Sophie said sinking into a chair. "Could you?"

"No, in fact he seemed quite excited about the opportunity to play such a variety of roles."

We then played Randy's tape and were both quite impressed with the quality of his work. Without appearing mannered or exaggerated, the three characters sounded quite genuine and interesting and indeed could be mistaken for women.

"For a homicidal maniac, he's really not a bad actor," Sophie said with a shake of her head.

We also listened to two of the other tapes. One was definitely superior to the other and equalled Randy's performance in believability and depth of feeling. I felt that I had found a real talent in this actor whose name was George McAlevey. He definitely would be an asset to the productions.

It was then time to call Frank. He answered his cell phone on the first ring and introduced me to the owner of the factory. "Hello, Mr. Blackthorn, my name is Harrison Hunt, and I want to thank you so much for helping us in this way. I understand that Frank has told you how important it is for us to determine if one of the voices I'll now play for you might have posed as Weezy Freemount to you. You know we're looking for a possible murderer."

"I understand, and I'll do my best to assist you," Sam Blackthorn replied sounding very serious and intense.

"Thank you very much, sir. I'll be playing you a number of tapes. Please let us know if any sound familiar."

I first held George McAlevey's tape recorder to the phone and played the three monologues. Mr. Blackthorn told us that he recognized none of these voices. I then played the second actor's tape. Once again this tape sparked no recognition from Mr. Blackthorn. In fact, he told us that this voice sounded more like a man's than a woman's. It was now time for me to play Randy's tape. Mr. Blackthorn said that the reading of the leading lady's monologue did not sound familiar to him. I then played Randy's performance of the ingenue's speech.

Before it was half finished, Mr. Blackthorn exclaimed,"That's it, I think. That sounds very much like the way I remembered Weezy as sounding. May I hear it again?"

With great excitement I played Randy's second monologue once again."That may very well be the gal who designed and ordered the snow globes for both Mr. Wetherstone and Miss Bogart. It's hard for me to state categorically that this is her voice, but it's very much like it."

My hands shaking, I effusively thanked the gentleman for his kind assistance, said a few parting words to Frank who promised to get back to us tomorrow after he visited the orphanage, and hung up the phone.

Ten minutes later, after saying good night to postmaster Seagull, I quietly sat next to Sophie for a moment before I softly said to her, "Well, the two people who've heard the imposter's voice feel that Randy could be our man."

"You mean our girl, don't you?" Sophie said with stinging sarcasm. "Now let's make sure that scumbag gets what he deserves. It's probably time to go to the police, don't you think, boss?"

There was a pause before I responded, and Sophie found it difficult to hear my response which was: "After we learn what Frank uncovers at the orphanage tomorrow, we'll do what's best for us to do." Sophie looked at me a bit strangely. "I've never heard that tone in your voice before, Harry."

I was unable to answer her.

CHAPTER

35

SOPHIE WAS RIGHT. SHE HAD correctly noticed an unusual tone in my voice. Unusual, because I was feeling an emotion that was certainly an uncommon one for me. And that emotion was *self-doubt*. A nascent nagging feeling that I might be wrong, that I might have rushed to judgment too quickly, that all my oh-so-clever sleuthing and deductive reasoning might not have been as ingenious or logical as I had thought.

And the seeds of this sudden and rare (at least for me) feeling of uncertainty had been planted only minutes ago during my phone conversation with Silverheels Seagull. When I played Randy's second monologue to him, the postmaster had immediately commented, "Hey, man, that voice sure sounds like that Weezy chick. In fact, it sounds more like her than she does, if you know what I mean. It's as if I were listening to her talking while I was dropping some acid, you know? It's realer than real, if you get my drift."

And I did somehow get his drift. I had asked the actors to think of women they knew and try to represent them while performing the monologues. Randy's first monologue depicting the glamorous leading lady could easily have been his impression of Bitsie Adams, the *grande dame* of Brookfield society who was an active and vocal member of the

Barn Theater's Board of Directors. He certainly couldn't have missed her dynamic presence at the dinner party Friday night at which he had worked.

The voice of his third monologue character sounded a lot like the warm, blue-collar tones of Joey Patowski. Whether or not he knew her from the Home Depot where she worked, he had been bound to know her from shows in which he had performed previously at the Barn Theater. Joey had designed lights there for years.

Randy's second monologue had not only sounded very familiar to the two men; it had also sounded familiar to me. But aggravatingly I couldn't put my finger on who the source was.

This disturbing feeling of doubt continued to gnaw at me as Sophie and I left the theater and drove back to Pemberley Cottage. Sophie questioned my silence during the ride, but I accounted for it by telling her I was feeling immensely fatigued from all that had happened today. Whether or not she bought this explanation was another story.

During the light but tasty dinner Louise served us, I would only tell the Freemounts that the callbacks had proved helpful in our investigation, and that we hoped to receive more information tomorrow that would tie all the pieces together. After the Freemounts had gone up to bed, Sophie expressed her surprise that I had not mentioned our suspicions about Randy to Louise and Augie. Begging the question by merely uttering "After all, my dear Sophie, tomorrow is another day," I quickly climbed the stairs to Tara. Muttering to herself that she knew more about birthing babies than she did the mystifying mood swings of certain New York City directors, Sophie soon followed suit and made an early night of it.

I, however, had a tough time falling asleep. My mind continued to race. Everything now seemed to pose nagging, unanswerable questions. What hard evidence did we really have to accuse Randy Williamson of murder? What really happened to Charlie at the bungalow? Did Louise really have a child who survived? Did that child grow up to be Randy? If so, why would he want to kill his father or Robert Gregory? What really happened at the Animal Shelter? I looked once again at this morning's *Brookfield Bugle* and intensely went over every word of the story covering Robert's murder. Something nagged at me about this as well, but once again it titillatingly remained just outside of my conscious grasp. I took out the mini recorder and listened to Randy's tape again and again. The voice that he used for the second monologue was so temptingly and frustratingly familiar. Who was she?

I restlessly tossed and turned until I said to the twelve male actors, "Speak the speech, I pray you, as I pronounced it to you, trippingly on the tongue: but if you mouth it, as many of your players do, I had as lief the town-crier spoke my lines."

"Remember us!" the three blood-stained bodies of Luke Halpert, Robert Gregory and Charlie Wetherstone moaned in ghoulish unison.

I turned to Sophie and said, "There is a play to-night. One scene of it comes near the circumstance which I have told thee of our Charlie's death. I prithee, when thou seest that act afoot, even with the very comment of thy soul observe yon Randy: if his occulted guilt do not itself unkennel in one speech, it is three damned ghosts that I have seen, and my imaginations are as foul as Damian Devoe's poison pen."

As I said the word *unkennel*, Hazel appeared holding the sweet tempered and smiling Lucy on a smart new leash that still had the tag "Made in Denmark" attached to it. Suddenly Randy began his second monologue, and Lucy began growling and snarling at the sound. A motorcycle roared through the room as all the lights suddenly went out, and from the impenetrable darkness we heard a voice cry: "Give me some light: away!" Everyone then shouted, "Lights, lights, lights!" A thousand flashbulbs then illuminated the face of the person who had made the cry.

And as I sat up in bed sweating like a pig with my heart pumping a mile a minute, I thought I knew who the murderer was. As I turned on the light and tried to catch my breath, the Player King's words from "The Mousetrap" came to my lips: "'tis a question left us yet to prove."

Although it was barely seven in the morning, I then reached for my cell phone and made two calls. I usually detested automated phone messages, but this time the recorded voice (which incidentally could have been a kissing cousin of Mandy's) proved most helpful to me. I actually reached a live person on my second call and after a quick but (if I must say so myself) brilliant bit of subterfuge I obtained the corroborative information I had sought. I now was actually tingling with excitement as I observed that the debilitating self-doubt I had experienced last night was thankfully beginning to dissipate.

I quickly dressed and went downstairs just in time to say a quick hello to Louise as she headed out the front door to her studio. I was delighted to see that no trace of residual resentment remained and warmly returned her cheek peck. As I entered the kitchen, Augie was concluding a conversation with the hospital on his cell phone. "Good morning, Harry. You'll be interested to hear that Belinda's condition seems to have improved a bit this morning. The drugs may have finally begun to kick in. This may be an opportune time for old Judge Griffin to meet with her. When I spoke with him the other day, he agreed with your point that Belinda's legal rights must be protected and said he'd gladly see her whenever she was able.

"I am so glad to hear that, Augie. I only wish I could get in there to see her as well."

"Why don't you come with me now to the hospital, and we'll see what we can arrange?"

I thanked Augie profusely and while he made a call to Judge Griffin, I scribbled a note for the still-sleeping Sophie and left it on the kitchen table. It read:

I think it was William Blake who said: "It is easier to forgive an enemy than to forgive a friend." Perhaps you'd be kind enough to make the additional effort to forgive my boorish behavior of last night. I'll try to explain all when you give me a call. I'm off to the hospital with Augie now in the hopes I may be able to speak to Belinda.

A Repentant HH

On our way to the hospital in his car, Augie explained a bit about Belinda's condition. Post-traumatic stress disorder changes the body's response to stress by affecting hormones and chemicals that carry information between the nerves. Having been exposed to trauma in the past increases the risk of PTSD. He rattled off a list of the classic symptoms of this terrible disorder many of which Belinda exhibited. When he mentioned recurring nightmares, I wondered if I might also have been affected in a somewhat similar but lesser degree by the tragic occurrences of the past few days.

I had an image in my mind of old Judge Griffin as a cantankerous Lionel Barrymore-esque figure: rumpled and craggy, ornery but tender-hearted, a quick-tempered but sagacious Oliver Wendell Holmes. That image quickly burst when we parked at the hospital's front entrance, and I saw the suave, debonair, classically handsome silver-haired *bon vivant* in the Armani suit and plum-colored waistcoat emerge with a spring in his step from his red Ferrari.

Bertie Griffin's firm shake almost crushed my hand when Augie introduced me to him. In the hospital cafeteria where we all had some coffee and toast, we worked out our strategy. Judge Griffin made a quick call to his "old golfing buddy" Brookfield's district attorney who with only a little pressuring granted Bertie's request.

The three of us took the elevator to the third floor. As Augie and the judge walked over to the uniformed policeman guarding Belinda's room, my cell phone rang. It was Sophie who quickly thanked me for my note and then told me a fax from Frank Gerrardi had just arrived, and, in her words, "It's a lulu!" She briefly summarized its contents to me. That excited tingling I had felt earlier this morning returned in full force, and I asked Sophie to bring the fax over to the hospital as soon as she could. I instructed her to drive my rental car over here as I thought Mandy's services might shortly come in very handy.

The cop looked a little confused as he informed Judge Griffin that he had just received a call from the D.A. authorizing Belinda's attorney and his clerk to meet with their client. And so a minute later we were in the hospital room, and I saw her.

She looked so tired and so pale and so alone. I wanted to take her in my arms and tell her everything was all right, that she would never again be alone. But all I said when she slowly opened her still beautiful royal blue eyes was, "Good morning, Belinda."

"Oh, Harry," she softly said. "You *are* here. I thought I had dreamed that you had come back into my life again. I've had so many confusing dreams lately. I even dreamed that my Robert was…"

As she began to remember what had happened to her brother, her rate of breathing began to increase and her eyes began to widen in fear. Augie then took her hand and calmly and reassuringly said, "We know that you don't want to think about Robert, Belinda. We know how painful it is for you to do that. But we've talked about how much better and stronger you'll feel if you try to remember even a few details. Harry and Judge Griffin want to help you, but they will need to know what you saw before they can help. The medicine that you've been given has reduced some of your anxiety. You seem much more in control than you have been the last few days. I think you can find the strength and the courage to tell Harry what happened."

"Try, Belinda, please," I said taking her other hand. "You can stop whenever you need to. We want to help you so much, but we won't be able to unless you try to tell us what happened. Please."

Looking into my eyes, Belinda slowly nodded and began the painful process of remembering. Haltingly, she told us that she had gone to the hospital Monday morning to take her brother home. She had brought clean clothes for him to wear. At the hospital she found that Robert had already been discharged, and, in a note he left for her, he told her that he had been so eager to leave the hospital that he was going to call a cab and go to the Animal Shelter by himself to see how Lucy was getting on. He felt he owed it to "that nice Mr. Hunt." He asked her to meet him there. She then drove to the Shelter and "found Robert, found Robert with..."

She had started perspiring heavily and her voice grew raspy, but she forced herself to continue. "I ran away till I found a place where I could get help. I called..." and then she looked imploringly at me. "You called *me*, Belinda," I said, "because you thought I could help you. And I will help you. I will. I promise. You mentioned a twin, an evil twin I believe?"

"Yes, Harry. That *is* what I saw at the Shelter. Robert was in his T-shirt and someone who looked just like him, who looked like his twin, his hooded twin, was wearing Robert's hooded sweatshirt, and there was blood everywhere. And Robert saw me and screamed for me to run, run away and get help, and so I did. I ran away from the hooded twin and then called you. And when I saw him, the twin wearing the hood, ride by on his motorcycle outside the window, I knew Robert was now alone. So I went back there but couldn't find Robert. He wasn't near the little dog any more, but I saw the blood and followed it till I found him lying on the ground, and I held him. I held him. I held him in my arms, but he wouldn't move, he couldn't move. My poor, sweet Robert…"

Her sobbing grew so intense that Augie asked the judge and me to leave the room while he attended to Belinda. Sophie was waiting outside.

"How is she, Harry?" she asked.

"Oh, Sophie, she has gone through so much. And I just made her relive it all over again. Augie said this would be a turning point for her. I hope so, but it hurt her so much to do it."

While I tried to regain my composure, Judge Griffin introduced himself to Sophie and told her that now that he had heard Belinda's statement of what she had observed at the scene of the murder, he could begin formulating her defense.

"She might not need one, Judge," I said as I walked over to them. "I'm now very sure who the real murderer is, and I think I know the way to prove it."

➤ ◆

I told Sophie to wait outside as a lookout while I used her pocket knife to cut a large enough opening in the screen door to allow me to enter. The living room seemed normal enough, but when I opened the bedroom door I let out a triumphant gasp. It was all here, all the proof we needed to convict this maniac.

On every wall hung photographs, hundreds of photographs. There was a candid shot of Charlie at the Oregon pound seven years ago when he had adopted Lucy and another horrifying one taken the other day in the bungalow showing the white gloved hand of the photographer holding a gun next to Lucy's head while Charlie was forced to drink from a full bottle of scotch. There was a shot of Louise and Augie at the hotel restaurant on their first date. There was a candid shot taken three years ago of Luke Halpert lying in a motel bed holding his arms out for the photographer to join him. There were photos taken for the *Brookfield Bugle*: several shots of Lucy baring her fangs at the Animal Shelter last Monday and one taken earlier this summer of the lifeless body of the theater's former technical director emerging through the shattered windshield of his wrecked car.

And there were photos of me. In one, I was wearing for the first time the cashmere sweater I had received as an anonymous gift from, I had vainly thought, a secret admirer. Another was taken last Saturday as I left my room at the Inn proudly carrying the new leather briefcase that had been anonymously sent to me the day before.

There were copies of the designs for all the snowglobes: the six sent to Charlie and the twenty or more sent to Sister Gretchen. There were the torn pages of the magazines and newspapers missing the letters used in Louise's birthday card. And given prominent space on a wall was a handsomely framed photostat of the adoption records, another copy of which Frank had faxed to me a half hour ago. And below this stood a faux marble pedestal atop which was placed what I assumed was Charlie's laptop with a kitchen knife imbedded in its cover.

Each photograph was captioned with all the details a prosecutor could ever need to convict the murderer to a life sentence. And then I found the diary. I looked randomly at only a page or two before I felt like vomiting. I was gearing myself up to read more of it when I heard the shots.

I ran out the door and saw Sophie lying on the sidewalk bleeding. Before I could run to her, she sat up and screamed to me, "Harry get in the car and call the police. Hurry, she's coming back!" The sound of the motorcycle roaring behind me prompted me to follow Sophie's advice. I entered my car through the passenger door which strangely refused to close completely behind me. "Oh God," I thought, "the car's been broken into." I immediately saw what had been stolen: the cell phone I foolishly had left on the front seat.

Before I could think what to do next, the killer made the decision for me. A bullet smashed through the back passenger side window. Looking out the windshield I saw that Sophie had almost completely crawled behind the house. Deciding to use myself as a decoy, I quickly started the car and sped away watching the familiarly helmeted motorcyclist instantly following me. "All right, you scumbag, I'll lead you right to the police station." I reached to punch in that destination on the GPS when I noticed with alarm that not only had my phone been taken but Mandy as well!

I tried to concentrate on how to get from this section of the city to the police station but was not having much luck, particularly because I heard and felt bullets splintering into the back of the car from time to time. As I looked through the rear mirror, the sight of the deranged cyclist following closely behind me was an exact reverse angle of the time Frank and I followed this cycle on that wild chase. And thinking of that gave me an idea. I thought I saw a sight I recognized and made an impossibly high speed right turn onto a dirt path. The car bounced madly as it climbed to the top of the path. With a frantic effort I pulled up the emergency brake with all my strength and after scarily skidding several feet into a new position, somehow, mercifully, the wheels locked and the car stopped only a few feet before falling back over the hillside. I got out of the car and noticed I was standing only a foot or two from the edge. I looked over the other side and saw where the package holding the snow globe had been thrown.

I held my breath. Everything was still. Evidently the murderer had missed the turn and had not followed me up the dirt path. The tremendous relief I felt only lasted a moment or two when I heard the roar of the cycle as it started climbing once again up the extremely steep grassy slope.

The cycle made a horrifying noise as it rapidly climbed upward at high speed. The second it was about to reach the apex of the hill, I released the hand brake and pushed my car back down onto the approaching cycle. I'll never forget the confluence of sounds I then heard: the crash of the two vehicles colliding with each other mixed with the frightened human scream. That scream continued as the cyclist free fell down to the bottom of the hill moments before the motorcycle and car fell on top of her.

I raced down as fast as I could. Only the head could be seen protruding from the wreck. I had a hard time removing the helmet but finally managed to do so. Meredith's vacant eyes stared through me.

<table>
<tr><td>CHAPTER</td></tr>
<tr><td>36</td></tr>
</table>

AS I DRESSED FOR THE gala opening night party, I couldn't prevent my thoughts from returning to many of the myriad details we had discovered about Meredith Beekee's strange and tragic history. We had known her only as the shy, easily embarrassed night receptionist at the Brookfield Inn. But astoundingly this had been only one of the many personalities she had assumed in her short but twisted and tormented life.

The page from the orphanage's records that Frank had faxed to me two months ago had stated that a baby born May eleventh twenty-five years ago had been brought to the orphanage by the midwife who had delivered the child. A notation indicated that the required form waiving all rights to the newborn had been duly completed by the mother whose name was clearly listed as Louise Mullen, age fifteen. The name of the baby's father was listed as Charles Weatherstone (sic), his surname apparently misspelled. The child's gender was clearly listed as female. When I had seen this, my hypothesis about twins seemed to be more plausible. But later that day I was to learn otherwise.

From Meredith's diary and from other evidence the police had compiled, we learned that the child who was christened Meredith remained at the orphanage for the first seven years of her life. These years were happy ones for the little girl who especially enjoyed her friendly and supportive relationship with the orphanage's director, Sister Gretchen Bogart. On her seventh birthday, Meredith was sent to the foster home of Roberta and James Beekee who later adopted her. The young girl's diary entries concerning her life with her new parents began as quite pleasant. She had loved the flash camera her mother had given her for her birthday. Since Roberta was a freelance photographer, Meredith enjoyed learning the mechanics of photography from her, and the two of them spent happy hours snapping pictures and developing them in the home darkroom. Soon, however, the child's diary revealed troubles at home. Loud, frightening arguments between her parents overheard by Meredith from her bedroom grew more and more frequent. On her eighth birthday, a violent fight witnessed by the child broke out immediately after her birthday party. A newspaper clipping stapled to the diary revealed that in a drunken fury James Beekee had fatally stabbed his wife in the chest with a kitchen knife.

From then on, the child moved from foster home to foster home, and evidences of disturbed behavior could be found in the ensuing diary entries, at least according to the police psychologist who had given testimony at the inquest. He had cited instance after instance of behavior and thoughts which he felt could be definitely labeled as sociopathic and borderline psychotic.

Although she expressed anger at the orphanage for allowing James Beekee to adopt her, she always remembered Sister Gretchen with warm affection and began sending the nun customized snow globes several times a year.

When she was eighteen and completely on her own, Meredith had obtained her records from the orphanage and then began a quest to locate her biological parents. She revealed in her diary that she never planned to confront her parents directly but rather wanted to be, as she put it, "a silent partner" in their lives. She secretly found out everything she could about them, devoting all her time traveling to wherever they were living and spying on them and their daily activities, always recording their lives in photographs.

Having learned that Louise would be attending a November Pilates convention, Meredith had taken a temporary job (one of scores she had taken while secretly scouting out her parents' lives) as a desk clerk at the hotel where the convention would be held. The moment she first saw him, Meredith had taken it into her head that the personable and good-looking Dr. August Freemount would be the ideal match for the still unmarried Louise. So she deliberately handed Augie the wrong hotel room key and hoped for the best. When her "matchmaking" had proven successful, Meredith knew that it was now her duty and mission to control the lives of her mother and father.

Eavesdropping on a conversation between Charlie and Hazel at a coffee shop following one of their Portland AA meetings in which they discussed how much Charlie wanted to get a dog, it was Meredith, one week later, working temporarily at the Portland city pound, who had helped Charlie select Lucy. One of the pictures Charlie had kept on his laptop all these years was a photo Hazel had taken of Lucy and himself at the pound. I got a chill while looking at this picture to see the blurred image of the teenaged Meredith staring impassively at them from the background.

Three years ago, the nature of Meredith's mission radically changed. She now felt the need to punish her parents for abandoning her and to make them atone for their amoral behavior in the past. Perhaps obtaining the file on "Stuffed Quail" from Yale had been the motivation for the new direction her obsession had taken. The new series of snow globes sent to Charlie and the baby items sent to Louise were the strategies she utilized to implement her new goals.

Somehow, along the way, I had also become a victim of Meredith's tangled and insane intrigues. The diary entries written three years ago occasionally accused me, as director of the Yale review, of "outing" Weezy to the world and therefore, in her mind, causing her parents to separate. Her revenge against me took the form of ruining any chance of happiness I or anyone close to me might have. Having read about my former romance with Belinda, and now reading about Belinda's return to New York and our working together once again, she devised the most devious of plans.

It was Meredith who had seduced Luke Halpert and had a torrid affair with him culminating on the night she had met him in a Queens hotel and had gotten him so drunk that he had taken her back with him to his townhouse. There, they had made love in the foyer and then when she heard Belinda calling out, Meredith had savagely stabbed Luke in the chest in the same manner that her adopted mother had been stabbed. She had then quickly left bumping into the chimes on the front door. This had been the "church bells" Belinda had thought she had heard before she saw the naked body of her dying husband stumbling towards her. Meredith had been disappointed when Belinda had not been convicted of Luke's murder but was delighted to hear of her mental breakdown.

Four months ago, when she read that I was a finalist for the grant and would most probably be coming to Brookfield, the town where not only her mother lived but Belinda was now recuperating under her brother's care, she begin to plot the details of her master plan to have final revenge on all of us.

It was Meredith who had caused the death of the theater's technical director and made it look like a car accident. Once again, her actions provided the results for which she had prayed when the theater accepted my recommendation to hire Charlie as his replacement. Soon both of her parents whom she deemed amoral and now hated, as well as the man who she felt had instigated their licentious behavior, plus the woman he loved would all be brought together in one place to receive their ultimate and deserving judgment. She moved to Brookfield and managed to obtain two temporary positions: night receptionist at the Brookfield Inn where I was planning to stay and free-lance photographer at the *Brookfield Bugle*, a job that might come in handy in carrying out her plans.

She had anonymously sent me the cashmere sweater and then, the day before I left for Brookfield, the leather briefcase in order, as she put it, "to soften me up" and inflate my vanity before I unexpectedly received the final blow.

And then, suddenly, Meredith's meticulously crafted webbed rope was in peril of unraveling. Charlie had called her from the road. She hadn't known that he had hired a private detective who had provided him with some clues about the sender of the loathsome snow globes. She hadn't known that Charlie had met Sam Blackthorn, found out about the orphanage and learned that he had fathered a girl a quarter of a century before.

When he had called the Brookfield Inn to ascertain their mailing address for the wedding invitations he would be sending Sophie and me, the person who had answered at the Inn had identified herself as Meredith Beekee. From his laptop journal, we learned that Charlie couldn't believe his good luck. Through some miracle, the daughter whose existence he had just learned was living in the town at which he would be arriving in a few days. He told Meredith his name on the phone and said he would like to meet with her when he arrived Saturday morning. She told him she knew who he was, and they had arranged to meet at the Inn when she got off work.

Meredith met Charlie in the Inn's parking lot. She told him she would like to have a long talk with him about the unusual situation in which they both suddenly found themselves. She suggested she show him how to get to the bungalow he was to rent and that they talk there. Charley readily agreed, and Meredith told him to follow her there. He asked her if there were a computer repair shop nearby where he could have the malfunctioning keyboard of his laptop repaired. She told him to follow her first to *Silichipz* and then onward to the rental property. In her diary Meredith wrote that she inwardly smiled at Charley's reaction when she got on the motorcycle. "This was the first of many surprises for him today," she chillingly wrote.

His computer dropped off at *Silichipz*, Charley followed Meredith up to the bungalow. When he parked his van and took Lucy inside, Meredith took the bag off the back of the cycle and then followed them in. The diary entry about how she had held a gun first on Charley and then on Lucy was harrowing to read. The abuse she hurled at her father, the threats she made about what tortures she would inflict on the dog and then on his fiancée if Charley failed to follow her orders sent shivers down my spine. After she had forced him to drink a full bottle of scotch, she instructed him to climb up the slope in back of the house and then cocked the trigger she had been holding on the leashed Lucy's head. "The licentious imbecile had pleaded with me not to hurt his precious Lucy," she had written. "He cared more for the damned dog than he ever had about his own daughter. I loudly laughed as I made the monkey jump."

She knew before she clambered down the hill that he had instantly died when his head hit a rock in the creek. She took the other liquor bottles she had brought with her and planted the incriminating evidence in the bungalow and in the van. "I hadn't laughed so much in years. Once again God was with me!" was her final entry for that day.

When she found that Sophie, Hazel and Frank had beat her to the computer shop and the UPS store, Meredith had followed them to the funeral home where she stole the laptop and the package containing her latest snow globe from Sophie's car before leading Frank and me on the high speed chase.

Meredith's written explanation of what had happened at the Animal Shelter promptly elicited a heartfelt apology from the police to Belinda, a quick resolution of the Robert Gregory murder case by the district attorney, and a verdict of justifiable self defense for me at the inquest held to investigate Meredith's death.

After she had learned Lucy had been taken to the Animal Shelter, she had called Damian Devoe and asked if she could accompany him and the reporter there to take photographs of the dog. She had arrived by motorcycle which she parked quite a distance from the Shelter's normal parking area. She had met the men and accompanied them to the exercise area when Rory took the dog there. Recognizing Meredith from what had happened two days before at the bungalow, Lucy snarled and tried to attack her. It was this picture that had appeared in Tuesday's paper and had nagged at me ever since. The sweet tempered Lucy had only acted this way once before. I began to have suspicion about the person who had taken the picture whom Rory had identified as a woman.

When the newspapermen left the exercise area to return to their cars, Meredith had pretended to go back to the cycle, but instead had doubled back and was about to finish Lucy off when Robert Gregory had arrived and shouted at her to stop. Recognizing him as Belinda's brother, Meredith quickly thought of the perfect scenario: she would kill Robert the way she had killed Luke, and Belinda would finally have to pay for the crime. She always carried a kitchen knife in her bag; she always had since she was eight years old. She surprised Robert by stabbing him in the leg. She then pulled out her revolver and pointed it at him. Screaming with pain, he had taken off his hooded sweatshirt to wrap it around the bleeding leg. Before he could do so, they both heard Belinda calling for Robert. Meredith grabbed the sweatshirt and put it on hiding her face with the hood. After Belinda had run back towards her car in hysterics, Meredith had forced the bleeding Robert to walk behind an outbuilding and had pitilessly stabbed him in the chest. She had never felt so satisfied and calm as she rode the cycle back home to develop the photos for the *Bugle*.

About the motorcycle: Randy had been horrified to learn what Meredith had done when she had borrowed his bike during those five days in May. When she had shyly asked him to use it because her car was "in the shop," he had slyly suggested he'd let her borrow the cycle "for a small price." After he had received the sexual favors he had demanded from her, Randy had no idea how deeply he had been implicated in the murders and how he was now "added to my list of prurient males to terminate" according to a late diary entry.

Thinking about Randy reminded me that after I had finally identified Meredith as the source of Randy's second monologue I had made two early morning phone calls...

A knock on the door interrupted my musings. I shuddered one final time and admitted Sophie who announced that everyone was waiting to see me. She was still hobbling around a bit on crutches but, thank the gods, had not been seriously wounded in the shooting. I smiled at her, and as I walked from the green room to the theater's lobby I thought once again how grateful I was that Sophie was still in my life.

Thunderous applause greeted my entrance. Everyone indeed was there. With a bow to the waist I acknowledged the cast who had at today's matinee and evening performances beautifully performed both of the two plays now officially in repertory for the remainder of the summer.

By the way, one result of my "Mousetrap" ploy for obtaining Randy's voice on tape was that I had decided casting both plays with an all male cast. This choice had been very well received.

I made the extra effort of shaking George McAlevey's hand. He had admirably taken the leading roles I had originally planned for Randy Williamson. I had agreed with Sophie that Randy's behavior had not warranted him a place in the productions which I had heard on the grapevine had been greeted by the critics, both the New York press and the local rather discriminating *Bugle*, with warm acclaim. The official reviews would be out tomorrow. I was not worried in the least. During the two weeks of previews a number of Broadway producers had seen and very much enjoyed the shows. It looked like my new plays would have a life long after Brookfield.

And so would Belinda. She was there still dressed in black and subdued but, Augie assured me, well on her way to full recovery. I flashed a smile at her. I saw her still beautiful royal blue eyes light up. And hope filled my heart.

I returned the full smiles of all the kind people who had stayed tonight to acknowledge the plays' success. There were Joey and Bill Patowski both of whom had performed their designing duties better than I had expected. Also there were my costume and sound designers and their partners. Their work had also been more than acceptable. I waved heartily to Anna Patowski, holding her husband's hand while waving back to me with the other.

I hugged Augie, Louise, Frank and Hazel. How nice that the latter two had flown back from Portland for the opening. I noticed Rory McClintock and Dawn the waitress from the coffee shop and Joe Flaherty from the bar in the crowd along with Silverheels Seagull, Bitsie Adams and Bertie Griffin. I was happy that Madge Magill had made the trip to Brookfield for the opening. Also there was Mr. Higgins the manager of the Inn who was still trying to find a new night receptionist.

I thought back to my early morning phone conversation with Mr. Higgins on the Wednesday we found the treasure trove of evidence on Meredith. I had called him at the Inn immediately after I had phoned the

Brookfield Bugle. The recorded voice at the newspaper had announced that the office was now closed but to press the star button to reach the voice mail of any of the paper's staff. The voice then read each person's name followed by his or her position on the *Bugle*. When the name of Meredith Beekee, photographer, was announced, I had hung up and called Mr. Higgins. I lied to him that I wanted to send a small thank you gift to his night receptionist and asked that he kindly provide me with Meredith Beekee's home address. With this information, Sophie and I found her house that I broke into. Unfortunately, Meredith had listened to my call with her manager on an extension phone and guessed my plan and had almost succeeded in ambushing us both.

My new best friend, Damian Devoe, was now fawningly seeking my attention. His glowing interview with me last month was even a bit too sugary for my taste. I nodded pleasantly to him and then looked at Lucy.

Yes, Lucy was there too and had flown back to Brookfield with Hazel and Frank. She also seemed to smile a bit as she received a tremendous amount of attention from the crowd. Charlie would have been so happy to see how well she was thriving. We all owed her a lot of thanks. After all, it had been Lucy who had tried to tell us who the murderer was. In addition to snarling at the photographer at the Animal Shelter, she had recognized Meredith's scent both on the motorcycle in the Inn's parking lot and inside the Inn where she had strongly sniffed it coming from the sitting room adjacent to the lobby where Meredith was working with Mr. Higgins. We had mistakenly assumed that it was at Randy that Lucy was so frantically growling.

Looking once more at Louise, I was happy that my fears had never materialized. She would never have to go through life thinking that a second child of hers had died, because what she had told us had been absolutely true. Only one child had been born to her twenty-five long years ago and had died soon afterwards. And that child indeed had been a boy.

After he had faxed me the orphanage's records, Frank had then located the midwife who had brought the child there. Lillian LaFleur was ninety-two years old when Frank had found her on her deathbed in a local hospice center. She was grateful for the opportunity at last to confess the truth after all these years. When Louise's boy had died, Mrs. LaFleur had used this opportunity to bring her own granddaughter's newborn baby girl to the orphanage and identify her as the offspring of the fifteen-year old Louise. The deeply religious family did then not have to acknowledge that the teenaged granddaughter had borne a child out of wedlock. The midwife thought no one would be hurt by this deception. Little did she know that four good people had lost their lives because she had chosen to save her family's reputation.

Oh well, enough sad thoughts. It was time to celebrate tonight's success and later announce that I was hard at work at writing a new play, a play about a young girl who was a wild townie near an Ivy League college and what happened to her and her illegitimate daughter. It would tell a multi-generational tale of a family tragedy rivaling the fate of the House of Atreus. I of course shall direct it. It's destined to be a triumph.